WORLD TAKES

stories designed to amuse
by

TIMMY WALDRON

WORD RIOT PRESS

Middletown, NJ
2009

World Takes by Timmy Waldron
A Word Riot Press Book
Copyright 2009
ISBN: 978-0-9779343-2-4

"Amanda" and "Worry is for the Well-Rested" were originally published by *Pindelyboz*. Versions of "The Gary Game," "Before Floyd Hit," and "County Line" were originally published by *Word Riot*. "Gravity alone would not hold her" was originally published by *Pequin* as "Gravity Alone." A version of "Sipping Soda in a Combat Zone" appeared in *Johnny America* # 5. "When it was good" appeared in *Elimae*'s December 2007 issue. "Things you would know about Paul if you were his friend" appeared on *Eyeshot*. "Coda" was first published in *Snow Monkey* #15/16, 2005.

Word Riot is a monthly online literary magazine dedicated to the forceful voices of up-and-coming writers. Word Riot Press is the print extension of the magazine, publishing chapbooks and paperbacks. For more information, please contact us:

Word Riot/Word Riot Press
P.O. Box 414
Middletown, NJ 07748
www.wordriot.org
www.wordriot.org/press/

Cover and book design by David Barringer.

Book was typeset in **Fairplex** and Futura.

Printed in the USA.

For Mom

With love,
T

"It is not a bad thing to settle for the Little Way, not the big search for the big happiness but the sad little happiness of drinks and kisses, a good little car and a warm deep thigh."

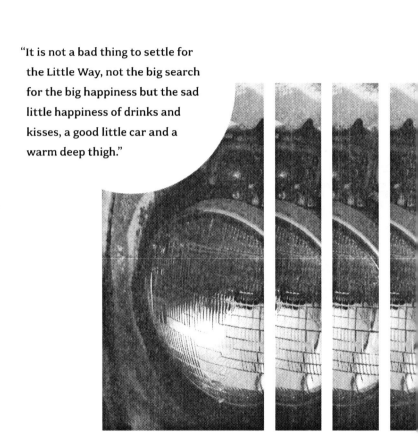

—from Walker Percy's *The Moviegoer* (1961)

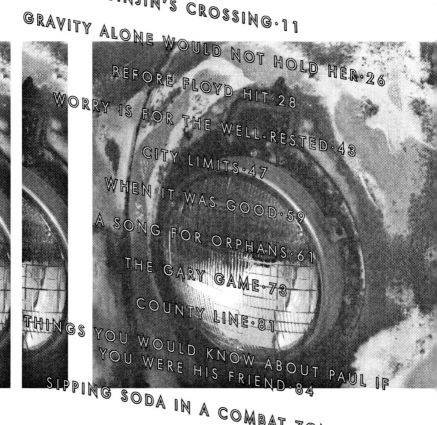

AMANDA

How many times did you trip and fall on that same piece of uneven sidewalk before you learned to walk on the other side of the street? By my count it is eleven, which doesn't make you the smartest person I have ever met, but whatever, you're good looking and that'll get you somewhere.

Remember all those restless nights of worry and tears? They really weren't worth much in the end. But hey, there were some laughs along the way. Remember that time that thing happened,

and we all laughed, and high fived? I bet you do, mainly because
your life isn't so great, and you sit up at night, in the darkness,
thinking up things to worry over. What's that all about? Inventing
things to worry about, it's a waste of time. But I guess that's what
makes you an artist.

The outside world, oh the big bad outside world, you can have
it. I'm going out to the desert for a while. There's a camp in the
wastelands that teaches you things about people and nature and
walking around. There is a lot of walking around. In fact, it is not
a camp at all, it is just a location. There is a large rock somewhere
in space and time. A tin can sits on the rock and I'll walk to it. I'll
take a black pebble out of the can and walk back. Once I do this,
I will feel better about myself. It is task completion. I will have
a sense of closure and a sense of accomplishment. The camp
costs eight hundred dollars. Which brings me to the point: could I
borrow some money?

I'll pay you back. It just might take me awhile. I started
worrying about money too late in life, I know. Here, take my
father's watch, he gave it to me before he died. Hold on to it until
I get you the money; it will be collateral. And I know what you're
going to say, my father's not dead. You've got a point, I'll admit
it. But I wasn't talking about actual physical death. I was talking
about the metaphysical death of the soul. The kind of death that
takes place after you buy a condo in Palm Springs, adopt a cat
and give your son a watch.

You know we can get it back, me and you. We can get back
to that great place, kings of the hill, where the air is thin and it
gets hard to breathe. And doesn't that make each breath a little
more worthwhile? Listen close: Hegel, Weber, Voltaire, Camus,
DiMaggio. Understand? Marx Brothers, *n'est-ce pas?*

I guess what it all boils down to is that I hate you. Don't worry,
it's not hate in its purest form. It is a lazy kind of hate, one that
uses very little energy and is not very time consuming: a Ron
Popeil kind of hate. Make the check out to cash and meet me at
the base of the mountain. Ride all night if you must.

SINJIN'S CROSSING

Sinjin Morann sat on the New Jersey bank of the Delaware
River late into the evening and periodically pulled whiskey
from his flask. Hundreds of dribbling creeks in the
Catskills and upstate New York came together in Northwest New
Jersey to form the moody piedmont that Sinjin loved to sit beside
and contemplate. At the end of a good think, the old man rose
with a bit of noise. The seventy-year old still considered himself
virile, but every now and again he felt the years in his bones.

"It doesn't look that far," Sinjin said. He picked up a smooth river rock and threw it towards the Pennsylvania bank. He lost sight of it in the dark and the plunk of the thing was masked by the rushed water of Scudder's falls.

Sinjin turned from the river and started his way back home. When the mood struck him, as it did this particular night, Sinjin would dress in a tri-quarter revolutionary hat, knee-high riding boots, long johns, and belted sword. The locals, who lived side by side on the river road, hardly paid the sight any mind. It was common knowledge in this area that Sinjin Morann and George Washington were one and the same.

"St. John Morann, I'm about this far from putting you in a goddamn home." Mary Morann, Sinjin's wife, held her index finger and thumb a quarter of an inch apart. She was twenty-five years Sinjin's junior and never let him forget it.

"Blow it out your ass, Mare." Sinjin hung his hat and dropped his sword in the umbrella can. "You're stuck with me."

"I must have done something horrible in a past life."

"Phahh," Sinjin dismissed her remark with a breath and a wave. "You don't know how good you have it." Mary turned to the fridge and opened the door. Before she could reach in, Sinjin was behind her, arms around her waist, kissing at her neck. The phone rang, causing the couple to groan in unison.

"You get it, I'll be upstairs." Mary gave Sinjin a mischievous wink then started to walk away. Sinjin couldn't let her go without one more squeeze. He pulled her back into his arms and copped a feel. "Sinjin!"

"Sorry, honey, I just love them titties." He gave her one last kiss before letting her go. Sinjin reached for the phone and caught sight of a note pinned on the cork board. He had to make an appearance at the Washington's Crossing Historical Reenactment Society next week, an annoying obligation he'd been trying to ignore. "Sherwood Forest, Robin speaking," Sinjin said into the receiver.

"Daddy, I'm getting married!" The voice bubbled.

"Who is this?" Sinjin asked.

"Daddy, stop it, get Mom."

"Mare, it's your daughter," Sinjin yelled. "She's gotten knocked up and has been forced to marry." Mare got on the line, immediately demanding that he shush and hang up the phone. Sinjin bopped out the front door and started a jig on the front porch. He didn't immediately recall what performance he learned the celebratory dance for, but he still had it down pat.

Even with the historical-reenactment society meeting looming over his head, Sinjin held himself in good spirits. His daughter, Sarah, who moved to Colorado the year before, would be home tomorrow. He was busting to see her. Sinjin was equally excited to meet his future son-in-law and test the boy's mettle.

"How do I look?" Sinjin spun around and gave Mary an eyeful of a well-dressed man.

"I hate that suit."

"You're certifiable. Larry Hagman gave me this suit and it still fits." Sinjin brushed a bit of lint from the sleeve and then glanced at himself in the mirror. What a sight, he thought, never had there been a smarter outfit. The suit was made of the finest Mohair, dyed white, orange, and black, with red checkered squares. "Not a lot of men can fit into a suit they owned thirty years before."

"It's just so…" Mary seemed to lose her train of thought while staring into the pattern of the suit. Her face went blank, then sour. She shook her head and pinched the bridge of her nose.

"It's so what? Out with it, Mare. I'm not going to live forever."

"It's just so busy," she told him.

"Where's my cobra-head cane?" Sinjin asked. Mary rolled her eyes in response. She picked her purse off the floor and pulled out a cigarette.

"Ah, there it is." Sinjin spotted the ivory fanged head by the dresser. Mary fished through her purse for matches. Before finding her light, Sinjin had the cobra head by her cigarette and pushed a button on the shaft to trigger a small flame from the snake's mouth.

···•··

"Take a seat, please." The meeting crawled to order in the basement of Our Lady of Good Council Church with the clack of Judge Randolph Rahl's gavel. "We have a lot to get through and a short amount of time." The judge, a short man, sturdily built, wore his dress robes at every meeting. Sinjin never much cared for Rahl's obsession with standing on ceremony.

Judge Rahl had erected a bureaucracy within the Washington's Crossing Society that frustrated many of the members. The rules were introduced as a way to give the society a longevity that would continue on after its charter members retired. Since the judge was the only one interested in the tedious task of writing up a charter, he became the head officer of the society. At first Sinjin was pleased with the idea—he wasn't going to do this forever. It was nice to know that the Crossing would continue on and become part of his legacy.

"Let's get this over with, Randy," Sinjin called out. Judge Rahl knocked his gavel and gave Sinjin a stern look. Sinjin replied to the judge by clacking the cobra-head cane against the basement floor and gave the judge his best set of bug eyes.

"I call the fourth official meeting of the Washington's Crossing historical reenactment society to order." The judge paused for a spattering of applause. He knocked his gavel in quick succession after indulging them.

"Is there any old business?" The judge's voice, authoritative, echoed through the chamber. "Good, then I'll get right to it." He stood up from his chair and opened a briefcase on the card table that served as his bench. "I have here the backbone of the Washington's Crossing Historical Reenactment Society." Rahl took out a piece of parchment and held it up for all to view. "This is the document that maps the way for future members and will allow our vision to continue."

"You mean my vision," Sinjin added. The judge's gavel came down in quick succession. Sinjin began to competitively bang his cobra head in response. The two escalated their racket until Mary elbowed Sinjin in the shoulder and ended the clacking crescendo.

"Mr. Morann, we are all aware that you started the annual reenactment thirty years ago, but I believe the crossing is General Washington's vision and no one else's."

"Randy, as usual you've gotten it wrong." Sinjin stood up from his chair and raised his arms with the cobra head in hand. Mary, having some idea of what was to come, sank down in her chair. "It was my goddamn idea to start these reenactments, and I've been George Washington every goddamn year for the last thirty goddamn years. The only reason you are not sitting in this basement alone, banging your goddamn pud with that goddamn gavel, is because of me and my goddamn vision." Sinjin's tirade was punctuated with brief bit of applause that died out before the judge even had a chance to bang his gavel.

"Okay?" the judge asked. "Anything else to add? Good. Before this meeting meanders any further I will come to the point. Section 4 of Article 14 in the Washington's Crossing Historical Reenactment Society Constitution states: 'No man or woman will be allowed to take a space on a boat if there is an inherent health risk.'"

"What are you up to, Rahl?" Sinjin stamped his cane in defiance.

"I am sorry, Sinjin," the judge said. "But I believe that, at your age, there exists a very real possibility that you would be at risk during these crossings. And God forbid we ever tipped over. Even with the rescue boats on hand, he'd be in terrible danger."

"I won't stand for this, and neither will the rest of the Society." Sinjin was on his feet. The judge put his gavel down on the card table and took a seat for the first time. "Your rules are hokum and everyone knows it."

"My rules are hokum?" the judge asked.

"Hogwash."

"I'm afraid the rules are perfectly legitimate," the judge responded.

"Hooey," Sinjin called out. He raised his hands in the air, like a conductor, attempting to galvanize the crowd, who sat half listening behind him.

"I'm sorry, Sinjin," the judge added. "I know this isn't easy to hear."

"Baloney," Sinjin sounded off.

"I'm afraid these safety ordinances are completely necessary," the judge said. "If it weren't for the new regulations, you would have floated away two years ago."

Sinjin shut his mouth and returned to his seat. He hated to think about the day the river beat him. There had been crossings that were canceled due to extreme weather. Sinjin felt no shame about them. But one year the river was very high; there had been a lot of snow up north, followed by an unusual warm spell. The snow melted and nearly caused the river to flood. The water was moving very fast, but it was so warm that Sinjin launched anyway. The boat was swept away with the current and had to be towed in by one of the Delaware River Rescue boats. It was a defeat that always gnawed at him.

"Rules are rules, Sinjin. It's time to step down."

"That piece of cat skin doesn't mean a goddamn."

"I'm afraid it does, Sinjin. It was notarized and is legally recognized as a binding contract with Mercer County's Department of Park Services."

"So what?"

"So, if we are in breach of this document, the Park Service will not issue us the proper permits needed to perform the reenactment. We will be barred from putting our boats in the water."

"You son of a gun, you've been cooking this up all along." Sinjin held the cobra-head cane up out and pointed the fanged mouth toward the judge. "I'm a goddamn bull. You can't tell me I can't cross that river come December. ı am an ox. Mare, how long did I go the other night?"

"Sinjin!" Mary's face went red.

"You tell 'em, honey. You tell them how long I went."

"Sinjin, sit down, now!"

"Forty-five minutes, Judge. When's the last time you went forty-five minutes?" The gavel came down again, louder and faster, with an anger to it. "Hell, when's the last time you had enough salt to get your soldier in the boat? Where's your wife? I'll ask her myself."

"I think that's enough," the judge added. "There's nothing left to debate. This crossing will not take place this year with Sinjin playing the role of George Washington."

"This is hooey. Who do you think you will get to replace me?" Sinjin asked.

"Well, according to the constitution, the next George Washington will be the member who holds the highest office within the Historical Reenactment Society."

"Would that be you?"

"I believe it would be, Sinjin." The judge fought his smile, but in the end it couldn't be masked. "If any of you have a problem with this and wish to resign, I understand. But I want to make this explicitly clear. No boat will cross this Christmas carrying St. John Morann."

Sinjin was fuming mad. He took his cobra-head cane and broke it across his knee. The pieces of his cane slid across the floor as he stormed out of the meeting.

Sinjin awoke in a sour mood. Everywhere his eyes landed sat reminders of his life as George Washington. His house, an old carriage barn built in 1765, had provided the first President with a place to sleep on one cold, snowy, war-torn night. The first thing he saw every morning was the mural he had painted on the bedroom wall. It was his take on the famous Emanuel Gottlieb Leutze portrait of the crossing. It depicted Sinjin as George Washington, and the boat was occupied with many of the actors and artists who had worked for him over the years.

Years ago, for much of his life, Sinjin sat as director of the Lambertville Music Circus. The reenactment started as a publicity stunt on behalf of the Circus. Sinjin's outdoor theater, under the big top, was regarded by some in the theater industry as a great innovation. By its own nature, the circus could only run in warm weather and it was not mobile. In order to keep the

Music Circus in the press throughout the winter, Sinjin started to reenact the crossing. Over the years, the publicity stunt came to the forefront of his endeavors and eventually eclipsed the Music Circus in notoriety.

Sinjin had always loved the crossing. He also loved the rich history of his home. But his love soured as the judge came to mind. The walls of his house held dozens of portraits commemorating different Revolutionary War battles in the area. He passed the battle of Princeton on his way to the john and scoffed at it. General Mercer was lucky, he thought, killed in battle, a hero's death. Downstairs, the muskets that hung over the fireplace gave Sinjin another pain in his pride.

"We're selling this craphole," Sinjin announced to Mary.

She poured pancake batter onto the griddle as he fixed a cup of coffee.

"If we're selling, I'm going to put you in a home and run off with the money."

"Not in the mood, Mare," Sinjin said, taking a seat at the kitchen table. "My kingdom is in ruins."

"It's not the end of the world."

"It's the end of my world." A car horn honked in quick succession, a sure sign of Sarah's return.

"Don't be so dramatic," Mary said.

"I'm an actor," Sinjin replied. He locked eyes with Mary and held her gaze. A pause lingered between them, his eyes glazed over with water. "Or at least I used to be."

"You've still got it, babe." Mary walked over to Sinjin, squeezed his shoulder and kissed his forehead.

"I'm on the back nine, Mare," Sinjin exhaled noisily through his nose. "I can admit that much, but I can't take someone getting over on me. It needs to be on my terms, not Rahl's."

"You old bull." Mary rubbed her hand up and down Sinjin's back. "You've got nothing to prove."

The front door flew open with a gust of cool air, and the whirling calamity that was Sinjin's daughter entered. She blew into the house with all the noise and commotion of a volcanic eruption.

"Daddy," Sarah dropped herself in her father's lap and gave him a kiss, then moved on to her mother.

"Mommy," she cooed before giving Mary a hug. "Everyone, this is Jack. Isn't he cute?" In the doorway stood a man obstructed by a wall of travel luggage and duty-free shopping bags. "Well, say hello, Jack. Don't be rude."

"Hello all, sorry for being a bit standoffish, if I could just put these bags somewhere, I'll give everyone a proper hello." Jack strained to keep everything from crashing to the ground.

"He's a goddamn red coat," Sinjin barked.

"Daddy."

"I'm George Washington, for Christ's sake. I can't have a red coat in the family."

"Sorry to interrupt," Jack stuttered a bit, suddenly a bit ashamed of his British accent. "But I'm either going to put this luggage down, or it's going to put me down."

"I can't understand a goddamn word this kid is saying."

"Sinjin, help him with the bags," Mary instructed. "I have the guest room all set up, you and Jack should have everything you need. And don't mind your father. He just lost his job as George Washington."

"Mare, that's none of the Limey's business," he scolded. Sinjin began taking bags and being as unpleasant about it as he could muster.

"Thanks ever so much."

"What? Don't you speak English?" Sinjin asked.

"He said thank you, Daddy. Me and Mom understand him."

Jack smiled politely as Sinjin grumbled something that sounded vaguely obscene on his way upstairs.

Christmas, as it tended to do, took its sweet time coming around, then darted to the finish line before anyone felt ready for it. The clack of the judge's gavel beat in Sinjin's head and fired his lust for vengeance. While Sinjin's public face was gracious in defeat, his private thoughts called for blood. He had been secretly meeting with former members of the Washington's Crossing Historical Reenactment Society and formulating a plan to bring the judge to his knees.

"Howdy, partner." Jack announced his presence from Sinjin's bedroom door. "Could I have a word with y'all?" Sinjin forced Jack to watch a countless number of westerns in order mimic an accent that Sinjin claimed to understand. Although the impression was way off the mark and would often be abandoned in mid-conversation, Sinjin now maintained he could understand the young man.

"Yes, come on in." Sinjin had his Colonial army dress laid out on the bed, freshly dry cleaned and ready for the Christmas morning raid. "What've you got there?"

"It's an early Christmas gift, sir."

"Give it here." Sinjin grabbed the long thin box greedily from Jack's arms. "It's about time you bought me something, Limey. You know, when you stay at someone's house, it's just good manners."

"Yes, well, hope you like it."

"Oh, my dear boy." Sinjin looked into the box with pure reverence. "How in the hell did you pull this off?" He reached in and pulled the cobra-head cane out, good as new.

"Mary told me what happened, so I went up to the church to see if maybe I could retrieve it from the lost and found."

"Genius, boy, pure genius." Sinjin inspected the piece closely. He put his finger on the lighter button then looked over to Jack with doe eyes.

"Go on, give it a try," Jack instructed. "Cowboy up and all that."

"Would you look at that?" Sinjin said with great glee as the fire emanated from the cobra's brass fanged mouth. "Makes me want to take up smoking."

"Glad you like it. I had them make the shaft from an Irish Shillelagh. You won't be breaking this one over your knee."

"Limey, this is a great gift." Sinjin walked to Jack and gave him a firm hug. "I'd like you to be on the boat tomorrow. I could use your help in waging bloody war against the Judge."

"It'd be an honor, sir."

"What?" Sinjin barked. "I didn't catch that."

"Yee ha, sir," Jack said plainly.

"Very good," Sinjin nodded. "Now make yourself scarce."

Early Christmas morning Sinjin met with his crew in the picnic area of Washington's Crossing Park. The men stood huddled around a smoldering grill at nine in the morning, clad in matching tan trench coats. The gang consisted of Brian Thomas and Gary David, both longtime members of Sinjin's crew, plus Peter Rice and Jimmy Watkins, who were part of the Delaware Water Rescue crew who saved Sinjin years earlier. Sinjin had forged a bond with the two heroes. Jack rounded out Sinjin's revolutionary pack.

The renegade group had picked a spot a half mile upstream from the judge's launch. From this point, the current would carry them fast, and they could cut off the judge's boat before it hit the New Jersey bank. Since the judge's gang had to launch and land from the same two points that the General charted back in 1776, Sinjin was given the tactical advantage.

"Alright boys, this is it, this is the day we have been training for. We all have different reasons for being here and not all of them are very good. But that doesn't mean we can't put our hearts into this. That worm of a judge pulled the rug out from under us, and it's time he got what was coming to him. Now I'm not going to lie to you. This is dangerous. The crowd may turn on us, and the water is almost freezing today. But I don't want you to think about that. I want you to stare death in the face and laugh. These are the times that try men's souls..."

"Sinjin, we know this part. We hear it every year."

"I was creating a mood, Brian." Sinjin unbuttoned his overcoat to reveal his smartly cleaned George Washington dress costume. "But, you know, let's just put the goddamn boat in the water."

"Everybody has a costume," Jack said. "I feel kind of out of place."

"Don't worry, don't worry." Sinjin walked over to his car and pulled a garment bag from the back seat. "I didn't forget about you."

"Thank you, sir." Jack wrinkled his brow and frowned once Sinjin revealed the costume. It was not authentic Colonial garb. It was a pirate costume and a pretty cheap one at that. "Is this a joke?"

"Of course not." Sinjin put his arm around Jack. "We're working with what we've got."

"I can't wear this," Jack protested.

"Put it on," Sinjin insisted.

"No, I won't. I can't"

"Rent's due, put it on." Sinjin held the costume in Jack's face until he reluctantly accepted the outfit. Once on, the costume was far from dazzling: a big black hat with a skull and crossbones, knee-high red and white striped socks, black pants tied off at the knee, a ruffled white shirt and an eye patch.

"You look great," Sinjin said. "I won't make you wear the parrot, but the paint-on mustache is non-negotiable."

"I look like a fool."

"Listen, kid, when I started this thing thirty years ago, all I had was a canoe, some friends in funny- looking costumes, and a fifth of Jack. Don't let the naysayers drag you down."

"They're getting ready to launch the boat," Peter called out.

"Let's move." Sinjin raised his cobra-head cane into the air and circled it over his head to initiate the charge. Brian pulled the tarp back revealing a smart-looking Delaware River Water and Rescue boat.

"Someone give me a hand." Sinjin struggled with a large canvas sack, filled with heavy steel chains.

"Maybe we're going a little overboard here?" Jack asked.

"Grab the other bag and those anchors," Sinjin instructed. "We're all in this together, thick as thieves we are." The rest of the men aided in the launch of the Water Rescue boat. There was no fooling around from here on out. "This is war, gentlemen, and I'm fixin' to win."

The Water Rescue boat was a bit of anachronism, but it moved well in the water. The boat also had had a few centuries of design improvements on the longboats used by the judge. Sinjin found the ends of each steel chain and locked them to separate anchors. He gave the chains a tug, then pulled the pad locks and a bullhorn out of the bag. He took a moment for himself, signed the three crosses of Saint Mathew, and let out a deep breath. The renegades were out on the river and in plain view. Sinjin looked over to the people standing on Washington's Crossing bridge. They had already taken notice and were pointing.

"Alright, boys, time to give the judge the high hard one." Sinjin stood up, placed his foot on the bow and took the George Washington stance. Sinjin cleared his throat and flipped the bullhorn on. It hummed in his hand and he smiled.

"Attention, patriots," Sinjin's stage voice boomed and elicited great cheer from the onlookers. "It is I, St. John Morann, the real George Washington." Sinjin rocked back a bit as the rescue boat picked up speed. The men had their backs in it. "I'm here to do battle against the tyrant that has taken my rightful place at the bow of that longboat. To prove my mettle, we aim to beat the usurper to the New Jersey bank and humiliate his efforts." The crowd ate up Sinjin's showmanship. Laughs and applause carried over the river.

"I think it's safe to say we're the crowd favorite," Gary said as he exhaled.

"Let's not disappoint." Sinjin took the cobra-head cane and pointed to the judge, then ran his finger across his throat. Sinjin's boat closed in on the judge's position, but the judge's boat moved well in the water. He had skilled rowers and a larger crew.

"I'll have you thrown in jail, Morann," the judge screamed. "I order you to back down and let me complete this crossing."

"In the spirit of our revolutionary fathers, I do not recognize your authority. Up yours, Rahly," Sinjin called through the bullhorn. The crowd continued to eat up Sinjin's hammy showmanship. "Limey, take a look at the bridge." Mary and Sarah had unfurled a sheet that read "Go Get 'em."

"Listen up, men. This is going to happen fast, and it's going to be messy. Prepare yourself. Before we all get knocked into the freezing waters, know this: you've done an old man a great service." The rescue boat slammed into the judge's longboat with enough force to shift the bow down river. The two boats floated side by side, locked in battle.

"Get to it, Jack," Sinjin ordered. The pirate moved to action. He grabbed one end of the heavy steal chain and threaded it through the rowing oars on the long boat. Once the chain was padlocked, Peter dumped an anchor over and sucked the oars from the long boat and down under the cold Delaware water.

"My hand," one of the judge's men screamed.

"Let me see," another rower insisted. The others circled around their teammate to inspect his condition.

"Don't let them take the port oars," the judge growled. His fiercest call had little effect on the men. The hired ringers could move the boat better than Sinjin's team, but they had no stake in this fight. Sinjin hooked his cane into the stern safety latch and pulled. The long boat began to spin. The river's current did much of the work. Jack looped the chain through the starboard oars.

"Help me, for God's sake. They're trying to set us adrift." The judge drew his sword and stepped past the crew. He was within striking range of Jack.

"Get away from my boat," the judge growled. He swung his sword at Jack's arm. Before the blade made contact, its momentum was stopped by the cobra-head cane of Sinjin Morann.

"Are you out of your mind?" Sinjin asked. "Compose yourself." Sinjin knocked the sword out of Rahl's hand. He jabbed the cobra head into the judge's gut. The quick poke took Rahl's air and forced him down onto one knee. Peter dropped the second anchor into the water and sunk the starboard oars.

"Paddle for shore." Sinjin stretched his arm out and pointed the way with his cobra-head cane. "The day is mine, Rahley. You can play hide and go fuck yourself all the way down river."

The longboat drifted down the Delaware River while the judge made a feeble attempt to paddle the boat with his arms. Rescue boats launched from the New Jersey and Pennsylvania banks. The band kicked up, as was the custom when George Washington landed. Sinjin and his boat mates raised their arms in victory. "I am an ox," Sinjin called over the bullhorn. "A goddamn bull, don't any of you forget it." He saw Mary and Sarah moving through the crowd. Sinjin jumped out of the boat and met them amongst the cheering crowd.

"My girls," Sinjin called with his arms open. He embraced Mary and Sarah and groaned happily as he firmed up his grip on them. Sinjin had landed on that shore as General Washington many times in his life, but this was destined to be his greatest and his last. The battle had been won and the war had come to an end, all on his own terms. The old man's eyes went glassy. He kissed each of his girls on the forehead then let them go.

"Come here, boy." Sinjin waved Jack over. "Next year, you'll be family, you understand?"

"Yes, sir." Jack nodded.

"You did good out there, boy." Sinjin hooked an arm around his future son-in-law. "I want you in the boat next year. I want you to keep George in the family."

"I don't know, sir." Jack took a step away from Sinjin. "I'm not sure this is exactly my cup of tea."

"Excellent," Sinjin said and slapped Jack on the shoulder. "Your training will begin in the new year."

"Sinjin," Jack put a hand on Sinjin's shoulder. "I'm not doing it."

"George Washington is dead," he said and took Jack's hand in his.

"I'm sorry, Sinjin. It's just not for me."

"Long live the new George Washington." Sinjin raised Jack's hand in the air as he yelled his announcement to the crowd. While only two or three people actually heard Sinjin, their cheer begot their neighbors' cheer, and from there the applause of the crowd rose like a swelling wave. Sinjin's eyes dried as he forcefully held Jack's reluctant hand high in the air. A new battle stirred in him.

WORLD TAKES | 25

GRAVITY ALONE WOULD NOT HOLD HER

We walked to the beach just after dark and sat ourselves in the sand. The dirty dishes, stained wine glasses, and general mess left by the dinner guests would wait until morning. We listened to the whoosh of the breakers and tasted salt held on mist wet air. These distractions were enough to keep us from our usual uncomfortable conversations. The moonless night lingered only a few moments before it appeared out of the water. At first glance, it looked like a giant red sail on the horizon. Its size and color made no sense in my mind. She was tickled by the sight of this and slid closer to me. She held my arm tight and sighed while staring at the glowing sliver of lifeless rock.

The moon pulled itself halfway from the water and began to take a recognizable shape. This ascension brought to mind the movement of the Earth and the pull of its rotation. As I watched the event, it became obvious to me that we were, at this very moment, flying through space at a reckless speed. She held me tighter, her nails dug into my arm, she could feel it too. By some miracle of physics, the beach we sat on and the moon we watched had never collided into one another. Now, such nonsense suddenly seemed entirely possible.

The moon swelled just above the water. She was on her feet now and then just her toes. Her arms were raised above her head, but somehow dangling in the air. It was as if she were a rag doll being carelessly held by child. Her body tilted towards the ocean. She was smiling, on the verge of laughter, but then something occurred to her. Her arms fell to her side. She turned to me and met my face with a much sadder expression. She started to move, toes dragging in the sand, her long hair blown back by the wind of her own momentum. I got to my feet and started after her, but she was already airborne, off the beach and over the surf. I watched as she disappeared into the moon, which was now a full bloody circle.

BEFORE FLOYD HIT

Ray Duffy's sunny disposition had all but burned out.
His life as a twice-divorced high school English teacher
had run its course. Things started to get to him, normal
things. Things most people considered part of their everyday life
plagued him to no end. There was his leased car to worry over.
Ray had already gone way over the agreed mileage, and there
were many more months left on the lease. And they had just

changed cable providers on him. He didn't know where any of his favorite channels were. On top of all that, there was the weather. It had been getting worse all week, not that he had been going out all that much of late, but still. The nonstop drizzling, overcast skies, and chilly winds were not the stuff of good moods but rather somber thoughts. Then there was his heartburn. He had recently developed a painful case of acid reflux that kept him up all hours, but he wasn't much for doctor visits. Restlessly awake, Ray started going to school earlier and earlier. He found that a few antacids and sitting up straight in his desk chair lessened the discomfort.

Finished with class work, with a fair amount of time on his hands, Ray let his mind wonder. He liked to imagine himself as the main character in the movies he loved. There were also a handful of real-life scenarios that could occupy his mind for hours. Ray sometimes imagined a scene where he verbally destroyed the dean for slashing the teachers' benefits package. The faculty would break into applause as Ray reduced their boss to tears. And then there was his smartass-student-gets-his-comeuppance fantasy. Ray would get out of his seat after a student had said something moronic about the work at hand. Usually this student would take the form of Gregg Noble. The muscle-bound smartass had recently started a rumor about Ray. It was whispered that Ray needed to take a special medication and wear a butt plug in order to combat uncontrollable flatulence. So Ray would dream. He would dream about walking over to Gregg, pulling him up by the shirt collar, and cramming his mouth full with Longfellow text.

On one terrible occasion, Ray caught himself pretending he was Walter Mitty, and it wasn't the adventurous side of the character either. He actual found himself imagining that he was the guy waiting outside the hairdresser's for his wife. That pathetic little fantasy managed to give him a sad bemused chuckle. Daydreaming about being in someone else's bad marriage seemed a bit too depressing to dwell on, even for the life-sick English teacher.

Sometimes, most times, but not all the time, Ray considered killing himself. He would think about gas ovens and long baths with toasters, cars left running in garages and high bridges over shallow bodies of water. In between such thoughts was Karen Lynsky. Karen was a new hire, right out of college, and she captivated his diminished soul. The simple question of what she would wear tomorrow seemed to be enough to keep Ray alive.

The rain pounded against the classroom windows. The noise grabbed the teacher's attention. It was 5:28 AM. Ray looked outside. It was still dark, it was still rainy…it was still this…and it was still that.

Across campus, Zero Sails opened his eyes and felt an uncontrollable urge to smile. The predawn light filled his dorm room and made every boring piece of standard-issue Rosehill Prep School furniture look interesting. Chelsea Peet stripped out of her clothes, climbed into bed, and was on top of Zero before he was fully awake. "Tell me when you're close," she whispered and then kissed him. "No babies," she added. This was the fourth time in two weeks Chelsea had snuck into Zero's room and woken him up in such a way.

"Okay," he agreed. Zero was always just a passenger on these expeditions of Chelsea's. He wasn't at all sure how to conduct himself and was even less sure what the appropriate high sign was in this situation. But, when all was said and done, the pleasure of it, the excitement that Zero felt, always overshadowed his nervousness.

"Look out?" He questioned more than warned. Zero took a deep breath, balled up his toes, and then closed his eyes. Chelsea clumsily attempted to get off him. When it was over, their sighs gave way to laughter.

"Morning sunshine," she said draping herself across Zero's stomach. "Have any interesting dreams last night?"

"Not that I remember." Zero looked out his window expecting to see an average morning. "It's really raining."

"Boring, let's not talk about the weather. We're too young to talk about weather." Chelsea's playful demeanor amused Zero to no end. Everything in her world seemed to be passé or boring. Somehow she managed to pull off her air of superiority without seeming superficial or snobby. Weather was simply boring. It was a factual statement rather than a matter of opinion.

"Ask me something else, or make a comment that will take me aback, something no one else in this dump would say to me." Chelsea grabbed a strand of hair that had been hanging in front of her face and crossed her eyes to examine the straggler.

"Why do you keep sneaking into my room?" Zero asked.

Chelsea stopped fiddling with her hair and uncrossed her eyes. She didn't have a quick-flip answer and that made him nervous.

"What? Too much?" Zero asked. He and Chelsea had been fooling around for some time, but this level of interaction with any person, let alone a girl, remained entirely new to him. *Zero* wasn't exactly a nickname born out of affection. It came from childhood taunts that dated back to his uncomfortably shy middle school days at Rosehill. It had stuck with him to this very day. The taunt "Zero fun, Zero personality, Zero friends, Zero Sails" hadn't been said aloud in years, but the name stuck and it became so commonplace that the teachers stopped calling him by his first name before he entered high school.

"Split ends," Chelsea told Zero and then bit down on the offending hair. "I guess I come up here because I know my father would find it very offensive."

"Are you trying to get back at him or something?"

"No," Chelsea said sliding off Zero's bare stomach. "He's a very nice man," she added. "Everyone loves him."

"Everyone? D-d-d-do you?" Zero stuttered slightly, a condition which had just recently started to afflict him, its onset usually triggered by a proximity to Chelsea.

"Of course, silly. He's my daddy." Chelsea, now sitting up on the bed, looked around the room. After finding nothing of interest, she blew air from her bottom lip and rustled her hair.

"So what about you? Is it true your parents sent you to the wrong house last Christmas?"

"They've got a vacation house in Utah and one in St. Bart's." Zero cocked his head, raised his arms, and stretched. "They told me to get to the vacation house. I picked the wrong one."

"Really? I never believed that one about you."

Chelsea's offhand comment gave Zero a shiver. He had sometimes assumed stories circulated, but he preferred to believe that people didn't care enough to bother.

"You should probably go," Zero said. He got out of bed and moved over to his dresser.

"Something I said?" she asked, draping herself across his mattress.

"No, it's just me."

"Boring," she sang with her hand in a funnel around her mouth. "What's the problem?"

"What other stories do they tell about me?" Zero asked. He moved over to the closet door and leaned up against it, his arms folded over his bare chest. "I mean, what do they say?"

"Stupid things mostly, but you really aren't always the topic of conversation. We 'normals' have other things to occupy our time." Chelsea pouted then sat up. She spread her arms and said, "Come here."

"I think you should go." Zero remained still, his back against the door and arms wrapped around his own body. He was serious this time and wouldn't give into her deflective charms. Once again, she sighed.

"It's not that I want you to stay gone, you understand," Zero said.

"I know, Zero." She grabbed one of his hands and tried to pull him from the closet door. He resisted. "It's okay." She whispered then mouthed the words *trust me?* Even without sound, he felt she had made a request rather than an ultimatum. She turned him gently from the wall and planted a long consoling kiss on the fleshy, overhealed crooked *Z* burned into his back left shoulder blade.

"Gotta run," she said and was through the window and out on the fire escape. Rain poured into Zero's room. It was quarter after six on a Thursday and still pretty dark.

From the South Dorms, Gregg Noble watched his girlfriend run across the quad in the rain. His buddy Trip had been in the bushes on a wake 'n bake run last week, and he saw Chelsea sneak up the fire escape into the third-floor window, Zero's room. His blood was boiling. Gregg believed Trip, but he beat him bloody just for knowing Chelsea was sneaking around. Gregg said if anyone else found out, he'd have Trip's balls placed in jar and put in the back of his closet. Her sneaking around was bad enough, but it was really who she was with that got his blood up the most. Of all the faggity-faggots running around this school, Chelsea ended up cheating with this little nothing, Zero. Gregg didn't care Zero had hit a growth spurt and filled out a bit. He was still just the same zilch he was back in middle school. Gregg would remind him of that, mark him up worse this time, and maybe carve the next Z on his forehead.

A quarter mile off campus in a faculty housing unit, Karen Lynsky sat on her toilet with her head in her hands and knees pressed tightly together. She thought about yesterday and how much she wanted it back. Yesterday, Karen's biggest problem was finding the right kind of outfit to wear to work. She always wanted to look professional. She was in a position of authority and the kids had to respect her. But those Tri Sig sorority days weren't that far behind her. She still liked to turn a few heads and leave them with whiplash. Ultimately, the professional side of things had more bearing on the day, being an educator and all. She still managed to look cute and find little outfits that provoked attention without discrediting her as a teacher.

Unfortunately for Karen, yesterday was gone and today her life was rotten with problems. Her fiancé had left her last night, no face-to-face explanation, just a note: "Those pictures from that party are out. I was sent a copy of them by one of the brothers. I can't marry you. It's too embarrassing for my family. Wish it didn't go down like this. Love, Alan. P.S. I heard that a bunch of guys from the old house have posted them online."

"Love," she repeated to herself. What an asshole. She was drunk, it was college, and Alan was the one who took the pictures. The whole situation was maddening and would soon graduate to morbidly embarrassing. Her marriage had been called off, and the invitations had already been sent out. Now she had to call and let everyone know the wedding was off. *"Just kidding, no wedding here. Why was it called off, you ask? Oh, well, there are these terribly personal pictures of me posted on Fratsluts.com. Alan and his family needed to protect themselves from any potential embarrassment."*

Karen lifted her face out of her hands, looked at the white wand sitting on the sink counter, and said, "Perfect." She repeated the words over and over. "Perfect, perfect, perfect. Nothing could make this day any more perfect."

"Channel 6 news will tell you what you need to do in order to keep your home safe." Karen listened to the weather report coming from her television in next room. "Floyd could be the strongest hurricane to hit the East Coast in almost fifty years, and it's heading to your area." Karen got up off the toilet and walked into bedroom.

"We will give you up-to-the-minute updates on the storm's progress." The sleek sexless anchorwoman on the morning news spoke calmly while flashing a bright concerned smile. Karen stared at the television, cocked her head, and made a face that would have sent her students running. She could hear the wind whipping against her building, but she'd been too preoccupied to pay it any mind. Karen looked around the room. The newscaster's warning faded to white noise. The place was a disaster area of reminders. All the trinkets, the bobbles, knickknacks and scribbled notes—just sitting there, reminding her, judging her. It was easy to leave, she thought. People who leave don't deal with the clean up, they don't deal with the mess. And that's what she was stuck with, mess.

"A flood watch is in effect," the news anchor spoke. "Harsh winds and torrential rainfall could be heading your way."

The television grabbed her attention once again.

"*Could?*" she repeated. "Open your window, you stupid dyke."

Karen picked her Tri Sig Halloween costume trophy off the nightstand and threw it through her only TV. Alan had noted in a post-post script that he had taken the television from their den.

It was quarter of seven on the worst day of Karen's life. She was stressed out, abandoned, embarrassed and now, according to the newly visible plus sign on the white wand in her hand, she was pregnant.

Ray leaned against the wall in the rear of the auditorium. The hall was half-filled with boarding students and a few lingering day students who arrived before bus service was suspended. Ray listened to the dean as he spoke. The governor had declared a state of emergency, and everyone would have to stick out the storm on campus. The teachers were to be paired up and take what remained of their first-period classes to locations designated by the dean. As the emergency plan became more complex, Ray tuned the dean out.

He had come to the conclusion that life was an addiction. No matter how bad it ultimately made you feel, you wanted a little more. And through the doors of the auditorium came his latest fix, Karen Lynsky. She seemed totally frantic, yet undeniably wonderful. Ray, the Rosehill king of unrequited love, swooned. He liked being in this place. Falling in love with women he didn't know was what made his last marriage last as long as it did. But Karen was a bit different. He talked to her from time to time and that had its drawbacks. The other imaginary love affairs were usually with women rarely seen. Like the pharmacist's daughter who worked weekends and holidays, or the Saturday morning bank teller with the long beautiful cornrows, and how could he forget the Amish woman from the Farmer's Market. All of them were indeed magical, but Karen was different. She didn't know it, but she had been keeping Ray alive for the last two months. She was his lifesaver.

Karen settled against the side wall of the auditorium. She bounced her leg up and down with the balls of her feet and nervously bit her nails. She wasn't certain, but she thought Ray Duffy had been looking at her. She ran her hand over her stomach. She couldn't be showing this early. God, she wanted to kill Alan for leaving. How could he have done this to her? He said he loved her, he said he wanted children with her. Now that she thought of it, he also said he wouldn't show those pictures to anyone. But still, even after everything he had done, she would take him back in a heartbeat. Everything would be solved. There wouldn't be any calls saying the wedding is off, she'd have a husband, and her baby would have a proper father. And how would she take care of the baby all by herself on a teacher's salary? And what if a student came across pictures on the Internet? God only knew how much those little bastards whacked off. Someone was bound to find them and tell the school. All those people seeing her would be awful. She'd be mortified. Karen would lose her job, and then she'd have no way to support her baby. Maybe she'd have to get an abortion. It would be the easiest thing to do. Plus, nobody would know about the baby. She could pretend it never even happened.

Gregg did his best to act cool while sitting next to Chelsea during the assembly. His only window of opportunity to put the fear of God into Zero was right before the students were split into groups. He didn't let on to Chelsea at all. He just sat next to her during assembly and pretended everything was on point. He caught her looking over at the little prick once or twice, and it really burned him up. It wasn't fair. How was she picking Zero over him? The kid didn't say peep. He just sat around the school like a lump all day long. He was just a nothing of a person, free to be filled with whatever stupid bullshit pleased her. That was it. It had to be. Gregg was strong-willed, competitive. He was going to an Ivy League school, for fuck's sake. And she hated that. She wanted a ball of dough to mold. She couldn't handle someone like him, headstrong and cut from stone. Gregg tried to make himself stop thinking about Zero and Chelsea. His heart rate was up and he could feel himself on the edge of a blind rage. The pills Trip scored for him probably weren't helping. They weren't pure steroids. He didn't want his hair to fall out or his balls to shrivel up. But the pills did have a kick. They had taken seconds off his timed mile, put a little extra torque behind his hits, and added fourteen pounds of solid muscle to his frame since summer. He thought they might also have been the reason he raped Janice Reece after the last dance.

The dean called the assembly to an end. Gregg and Chelsea were put into separate groups, which worked to his advantage. As the crowd shuffled out of the auditorium Gregg leaned over to kiss Chelsea. She turned her cheek to him. It was something she'd never done before.

"I'm going to go catch up with Trip, since we're in the same group and all," he told her. She nodded and moved away from him, her attention noticeably elsewhere. All the exits were closed except for the one left of the stage. All he had to do was hold up by the stage-door entrance and wait for Zero to walk by. Gregg would grab him and drag him backstage and have a little fun. He watched the kids as they shuffled out. None of the students noticed him leaning against the wall in the shadows of the entrance. Gregg got a little thrill from the whole scene.

Before bringing the assembly to a close, the dean announced which classes would be combined. Ray went white realizing he was paired with Karen. Ray would be spending the better part of the day in close quarters with his most treasured morning muse. It was awful. Ray didn't want to know Karen. He was happy just making her up. The real Karen wouldn't have the same medicating effect his Karen did. The real Karen would complain, nag and demand. She'd have real feelings and probably even used the bathroom. Ray looked at her and cringed. Why was her leg jumping so much? She was probably a raving lunatic, ripe with weird neurological ticks, problems of her own, problems she would want to share with Ray, problems that would need his help to solve. No, it was too much for him. Just the thought of getting to know the real her infected his imaginary Karen with terrible ordinary things. In a moment she had been ruined for him, his fix was gone. His stomach gurgled. A sharp dull pain crawled up his spine. He took a deep breath and fought the urge to clutch his chest. The students were out of their seats. Ray felt confined in the crowd of moving bodies and needed to be alone. He moved toward the backstage entrance.

Zero had no idea what had just happened. One minute he was shuffling his feet along with the crowd. The next moment everything spun around. He was slammed on his back and dragged through the dark. A key light had been left on backstage. Zero focused his eyes, then went white. It was Gregg and he had Zero's shoulders pinned under his knees. The two had disappeared behind the stage curtains, and none of the students cared enough to take issue with the sudden abduction. Zero started to shiver uncontrollably as if he were feverish.

"Hey, buddy," Gregg whispered in a measured tone. It seemed forced but nonetheless scary. "Word is you and my girlfriend have been sneaking around together. Can't say I'm happy about that." Gregg took a big snotty inhalation through his nose and mustered up a huge loogie. "My brother used to do this to me all the time." He puckered his lips and let a huge glob of snot dangle from a thin string of spit. Zero squirmed back and forth, turning his head side to side, but it was useless. The loogie hung, Damoclesian for a moment, and then dropped. "Oopsy." Gregg laughed. "My brother could hold his for hours. I guess I'm no good at it." Gregg became more serious. He reached into his jacket pocket. "This won't be as easy for you to cover." Gregg pulled out a lighter, then a pair of scissors. The scissors had been modified.

He ripped them apart so it was just one side, the handle and a shear. For all Zero knew it could have been the same one Gregg and the others used on him years before. Gregg put the lighter up to the point of the scissor and stared at Zero. "You remember how the drill goes, don't you, Zero?"

It was the most horrible scream Chelsea had ever heard. Guttural like a man's, then it went to a high squeal, almost a whistle. It sounded awful. Whoever it was would probably be better off dead than alive at this point. A few teachers cut through the crowd like the Secret Service. If anyone stopped to notice the look on her face at that moment, they'd think she was nuts. Amidst the terrible scream, packed in a hallway crowded with shocked students, she was smiling. Zero had really started to get to her in a way no boy ever had. She felt dorky thinking about him and being with him and what they would talk about next. These flowery thoughts *so* weren't her style, but she couldn't help it. She had fallen for a boy whom everyone at Rosehill either ignored or found fashionable to mistreat. To her it made the discovery seem all the more special.

Ray had escaped the crowd and found momentary relief backstage. After a few deep breaths, he realized he was not alone. There were two kids whispering among the stockpiles of theater props and set dressing from the plays of Rosehill's past. At first glance Ray thought he had walked in on some kids fooling around. Stories about the drama kids were well known. When he spotted the knife in Gregg's hand, he froze.

Ray had heard about the hazing that went on in the dorms but never thought it was as bad as rumored. It pissed him off, all this privilege, all these resources, all this attention, and still these kids acted like total assholes. Ray felt his heart take off. He crept towards Gregg. It was as if he had slipped into one of his daydreams. He grabbed one of the plaster-molded tablets used in the spring production of the *Ten Commandments* and moved quietly up to the boy. Before the bully noticed a new presence,

Ray slammed Gregg over the head with the tablet. Even before the screams, Ray realized he had done something horribly stupid. But he couldn't hold back his smile. It felt so good to act out. Gregg toppled over wailing. The other boy, who had been pinned to the ground, ran off. Gregg's shrieks sounded horrible. He rocked back and forth with his shaky hands clutching his face. There was no blood, and the knife was on the floor by his feet. Somehow Ray hadn't caused Gregg to stab himself. That was something, he guessed.

"Gregg, calm down. Let me take a look."

"He burned me, he burned my face."

"Let me see, Gregg." Ray pulled back the boy's hands and took a look. "You're going to be okay, son," he said. Ray had knocked Gregg's head into the hot lighter that the boy was using to heat the knife. The metal of the lighter landed on the flesh in such a way that the burn mark looked like a smiley face. It was square in the mild of his forehead. It wasn't all that bad, but it sure would leave a funny-looking mark.

"Okay, champ, on your feet." Ray grabbed Gregg by the arm and helped him onto his feet. "Let's get you a bandage for that."

There was no doubt in his mind that he would be fired for this. This would be a huge controversy in the school. It would probably make the papers. Maybe a lawsuit. Even though Gregg thought it was the other kid's fault, Ray would own up to it. The whole impending ordeal was just what he needed, a nudge in the right direction.

"Is everything okay?" Mrs. Masterson asked, a bit short of breath.

"Everything's fine," Ray answered. "Had a bit of an accident is all."

"What happened?" she asked.

"The damndest thing," Ray said. "Do you mind taking Gregg to get patched up? I'm going to have a look around, make sure no other students are trying to hide out back here."

"Yes, of course."

Ray watched Mrs. Masterson walk Gregg off the stage. Mrs. Masterson asked what happened once more. Gregg turned back, looked at Ray and then to the commandment prop lying on the ground. The boy seemed to be putting it all together. Once alone, Ray grabbed at a rope dangling from the rafters and gave it a tug. It pulled tight with no give. "Hmm," he smirked. "Not bad. "

"Keep moving," Karen repeated over and over as she fought against the current of students. She admitted, only to herself, that her interest in the scream was purely as a surveyor of a car wreck rather than of sincere concern. Once backstage she found her partner Ray Dutty fiddling with a stage rope. He gave it a substantial pull.

"Better be careful with that," Karen said. Ray was noticeably startled by her. He had the guilty look of a child caught doing something forbidden. "You might cause a sandbag to fall on someone's head."

"Sorry," he said and let go of the rope. "I was just checking." He pointed up to the darkness above the stage. "You know, for safety."

"What was that scream all about? "

"You know Gregg Noble?"

"Yeah," Karen laughed as she spoke. "He's constantly trying to discover new ways to look up my skirt and down my blouses."

"I'm sure," Ray laughed. "I found him back here picking on some kid. I wasn't thinking and smashed him over head. I think he had a brand or something. He ended up burning himself somehow."

"Are you serious?" Karen bubbled. "That is awesome." Karen's excitement reflected on Ray's face. He began to grin, shyly at first, and then a totally uncontrolled expression of happiness emerged. The smile came on slow. It was as if he didn't immediately understand her words. Only after the understanding did Ray find himself in agreement. *Why yes,* his smile seemed to say, *it is awesome.* He let out a solid breathy laugh.

"I've thought about doing that a hundred times, if I've thought about it once," she said. "You'll be a legend around here." Karen gave Ray a friendly, way-to-go punch in the arm.

Ray laughed again. "Yeah," he said happily.

"Well." Karen spoke after a lingering silence. "We better get moving." She looked at Ray. His eyes didn't seem to register. "You know, we're watching a group of students together, right?"

"Yeah," Ray said. "I mean, yes, of course. Let's get to it."

He had lost himself in thought for a moment, but it wasn't a daydream this time. Ray found himself reliving the event with Gregg, thinking about what he had actually done. He took a rare sense of accomplishment from the thought. It seemed, for just a moment, that he had actually been able to be the hero of his own life. A feeling long absent swelled within him. Ray followed Karen off the stage.

WORRY IS FOR THE WELL-RESTED

I'm in the boardroom downtown in San Francisco. I don't even remember showing up for work today. I hope they fire me, just like they fired Bill. Well, not exactly like that, that was awful. He was caught downloading a phenomenal amount of pornography. They did some calculation in OIT that showed he spent forty-five seconds out of every minute looking through smut. We all had to listen to Maggie, this Brit from Tech Services, talk about pornography in the office. After the meeting, they fired Bill. It was uncomfortable, even for those of us not involved. That was the last time I was in this boardroom.

The view from this room is fantastic. We're on the fifteenth floor overlooking Chinatown. Felipe walks into the room and sits at the head of the table. He's been the CEO for five weeks. The whole office is here. It makes me think this is an ambush. This might be how they fire me. Someone will talk about incompetence in the workplace. My face will burn red as they talk. I will adjust myself nervously in my seat, and as my pants slide across the leather, it will invariably make a fart noise. But right now I might be too tired to care. I'd be happy to go home and get some sleep. Unemployment's a worry for the well-rested.

I shouldn't be here. I should have called in sick. I look sick. I'd call out tomorrow, but tomorrow's Saturday. I can skip Monday and have a three-day weekend. Felipe starts talking about the Unicorp team and its global something-something. Don't sell it to me, pal, I work here. My attention drifts back out the window. The sky is so blue today. I should have keyed up in the bathroom before the meeting. I might fall asleep as is. Felipe's voice is so calming, constant and relaxing. I don't like doing that stuff at work—keying up, too unhealthy. Red Bull and coffee will get me through the day, and maybe a nap on the toilet. Yes, that's just the thing. And no alcohol during lunch. I should just eat something, I haven't eaten in awhile. I need to even out, this is terrible. After the meeting I'll grab the earthquake kit out from under the sink and take the morphine. That will help me get through the day.

"I'd like to convey both my sincerest thanks and deepest sympathies to all of you." Felipe smiles and nods before leaving the room. Everyone gets up and starts to file out. I've missed something here.

"What just happened?" I ask but should have only thought.

"We just got laid off, brainiac," snaps the woman I share a cubicle with. She looks like a pile of soft vanilla ice cream that has just started to melt. A handful of my coworkers overhear the back and forth and start to laugh. Some try to hold it back.

"Oh," I say. "That wasn't so bad." I don't know what I've been so nervous about. I'm going home and going to bed. Tomorrow, I'll start looking for a new job. I walk by my cubicle and straight for the elevator.

"Where are you going?" Soft Ice Cream barks.

"Home."

"It's not time to leave."

"We just got laid off," I say.

"You're an idiot." She shakes her head. "Didn't you listen? The office won't close for another six months. If you leave now, you won't get your severance package."

"I'm just in shock, I guess, because of the news." I stare at her blankly for a moment before continuing. "I love it here."

"Snap out of it and get to work."

"Are you supposed to talk to me like that?"

"Excuse me?"

"Nothing." I go back to my computer and sit down. Everything looks like it has fuzz around it. I hate staying up all night. Why do I hurt myself in such a manner? This has to be the worst. But, now that I think of it, it's not. The worst was a few months ago when I stayed up all night playing *Trivial Pursuit*. There was so much beer, so many cigarettes and all that cocaine. I felt so smart, we all did. I didn't even notice it was light out until I heard my alarm going off. I was still at the dinning-room table when it started to buzz. It was horrible.

Everyone at work knows I am a wreck. They have to know. How could they not? It is so obvious. Calling out sick on Mondays and Fridays, always late, always sniffling. And you can't wash that out-all-night kind of funk off with one shower. I place my fingers on the homebase row and feel my soul empty out all over my keyboard. I've corrupted myself. I am morally bankrupt and sorely in need of a nap.

I start entering the alphanumeric serial numbers into the database, but something seems different. My usual dread has dissipated. I'm still tired, a bit unsure of myself and generally frightened of the world, but I do not dread being here. I won't always have to work in this cubicle next to that evil lump of soft serve. This is not what I am going to do for the rest of my life. In a few months this office will close and I will be free from Unicorp. I won't ship toxic and noxious fumes to countries with non-existent environmental laws. I won't be passing gas for the rest of my life.

Felipe sends an email to the whole office detailing the last days of Unicorp. For the most part it is business as usual. Then there will be waves of layoffs. We will all get severance packages. I haven't been this happy in a long time. Tomorrow I will start to worry again.

CITY LIMITS

And when I wake up, I don't feel the doom. Everything seems a little better than it did yesterday. I walk over to my dresser, grab a towel and look in the mirror. Zelda has drawn a picture with her lipstick. At first glance, it looks like a rocket ship. There is a red line pointing to a drawing with a note that says, "I like your cock." This is what pride feels like.

There are a few quick knocks on my bedroom door before it swings open. My housemate JB stands tall and wiry with his hair a mess. He's in the suit he had on yesterday. His right nostril is caked with rust-colored blood. I smile at him, even though I have an overwhelming urge to slug him in the face. I want to open up that weak little vein hidden up his nose.

"Morning," he says.

"Morning," I reply. "Didn't make it home last night?"

"Something like that," he says.

"Anything worth telling?" I ask.

"Not really." JB leans down and sifts through the pile of mail that has collected underneath the mail slot of the outside in-law door and spreads the envelopes around on the floor. Once he finds his mail, he turns to walk out. I hear the shower go on upstairs. The line has already started. There's not much chance of getting any hot water this morning.

"You need to get that thing cauterized," I tell him as he starts to leave.

"It's the dry air, that's all." He turns back to me. "Who wrote that?" JB points to the mirror.

"Zelda was here last night."

"Nice," he says and gives me a pat on the arm. JB walks towards the door, but can't leave without making one last comment. "Objects in mirror may appear bigger than they actually are."

"Funny."

"Good luck on that job search."

"Thanks."

Martha

I have a list of ten temp agencies downtown. By my third stop, I pick up a job. Two weeks of data entry in the accounts-payable department of an insurance company. The job doesn't start until Monday.

The morning mist is burning off and very little fog remains in the sky. I head across the plaza to the Modern Art Museum. The line outside is long, but I have this special membership card. Martha had traded me and JB these MOMA Gold Cards for drinks a few weeks back. I think she was working in the coat room at the time.

I flash the card to the intern at the member's entrance. Her eyes light up. I'm escorted through the lobby and dropped off at the elevator. She thanks me over and over for my patronage. This museum was made possible by donors like me. I graciously nod and tell her, "It's nothing, really." I take my first twenty milligram cocktail of anti-depressants and brain drugs in the elevator. I'm now prepared for artistic stimulation.

There is a piece by Tom Marioni that immediately catches my eye. It's a refrigerator, an old one from the Fifties, and it's filled with empty bottles of Anchor Steam beer. The light fixture hanging from the ceiling allows you to physically be inside the piece. The note tag says this exhibit is the result of his performance piece called "The Act of Drinking Beer with Friends is the Highest Form of Art." Something he did back in the Seventies. It really speaks to me.

"You can't drink the art," a girl whispers in my ear and squeezes my love handle. I jump and let out a high-pitched squeal. People turn and give us sharp looks. Gold Club members don't act this way.

"Easy, Ethan," Martha says, looking embarrassed. "I didn't think you were going to mess yourself."

"You just surprised me," I say. My face glows hot with embarrassment. "What are the odds?"

"Pretty good, I guess." She mocks me with a crossed eyes and a scrunched face. "You know I work here."

"Hadn't crossed my mind."

"Yeah, right." Martha breaks eye contact and starts looking around the room. She should feel guilty for the way she treated me, but I see no signs of it in her body language or speech. "You didn't come all the way down town to look at empty beer bottles." She smirks. "You could have done that at home."

"This guy's a genius," I say, looking over Marioni's work.

"Let's get an eyeful. I'll give you the full Gold Card tour." Martha grabs my hand and leads me to the next object of her interest. She's like a kitten with ADD pouncing from one piece to another. As soon as something catches the corner of her eye, she moves towards it. Martha's got an opinion on every piece. Each observation spans the full spectrum, from unique insight to just making a raspberry at something. She is a bizarre bundle of energy that is endlessly fascinating. She's also cute enough to make me forget that she used me to make JB jealous.

"Let's head to my place and knock back a few drinks, you game?"

"Last time we did this, it didn't go so well for me," I say.

"Still a little sore about that, huh?"

"You left me at a bus stop." I lean closer to her and lower my voice. "I know about you and JB."

"I'm sorry, Ethan. It was a dick move." Martha touches a button on my shirt. That's all it takes, fiddling with a shirt button, and I will do whatever she wants for the rest of the day. She looks me in the eye. "Let me make it up to you. Pencils have erasers."

"Okay," I say dumbly.

A sense of relief hits me as we enter her apartment and find it empty. Martha tells me that her roommate Bobby just started working at a coffee shop downtown. He won't be back until later tonight. I watch her as she moves down the hallway. She drops her keys on the table next to the door and throws her bag into the living room. I remember overhearing her tell Zelda that she likes catching a guy checking her out.

"Want a drink?" Martha asks and then looks over her shoulder. I have my eyes trained on her ass. She smiles at me. I get a hard-on.

"This isn't right," I say to myself.

"What?" Martha calls back to me.

"Absolutely, a drink, please."

"That's what I like to hear," Martha responds. Music plays through the apartment. I recognize the song but can't name it.

"Hope it's not too strong," Martha says while putting the cold drink in my hand. She plops down next to me. This has happened before, but something feels different.

"I'm not sure if you heard, but Zelda and I are kind of seeing each other," I say.

"I know, she told me," Martha replies and then leans in and kisses me.

As I kiss her, my mind works. What kind of outcome can I expect from this? Who wins and who loses? Martha used me and tossed me aside for my best friend. If I have sex with her, I will have a win against her and we will be even. Similarly, JB has been running around behind my back with Martha. He went for her after I told him I was interested. Sex with Martha equals a win against JB. Zelda, on the other hand, might be a victim in all this. However, we haven't talked about our relationship, and it is possible that she is still sleeping with other people. In this case, sex with Martha offers me insulations from Zelda. As for me and Bobby, I'm thinking that's square.

Me and Martha do it on the futon and on the living-room floor. This feels wrong in the most wonderful way. My heart thunders as we fuck. I feel like there's a warrant out for my arrest and the police are at the door.

"Don't tell anyone about this," Martha says when we're done. She is laying on the carpet, bottomless with her back to me.

"I know the drill," I tell her. I put on my clothes and walk out the door.

As I make my way to the Muni, my euphoria is overtaken by guilt. Mine is the purest form of the stuff, a perfect energy, abundant and self-replenishing. I try to beat the beast into submission. As long as I've mumble something like "I hate me" or "stupid" almost loud enough for someone to hear, I've paid my penance for the day. I also take a pill for good measure. The real issues are pushed deep inside and then muted by science.

I stop in the library downtown. JB emailed me and wants to meet me at a bar I've never heard of. Zelda has also emailed me. She sent me a love poem called "Be my forever man." I tell JB I'm busy and don't respond to Zelda. I couldn't possibly look at her right now. I hate me. I am a bad friend. I need a bottle of water.

..•..

Zelda

We spend the entire day in bed, naked, in and out of sleep. We make sweet tender love, then go at it in a manner that borders on violence. It rains most of the day, and the drops against my window are the only sounds we hear besides our own. The house above me is empty. My roommates, their friends, and the ruckus that comes with them are absent and unmissed. As we lay there, in the quiet, Zelda tells me I feel like home. I might not mean it, but I tell her the same. I should be happy here with her, but somehow I am bored. My heart always beats at the same tick-tock rhythm when we are together. The day is gray and overcast. It slips unnoticed into night. We wake up in the morning, shower together, and then get dressed.

"Is that insurance company using you again this week?" Zelda asks.

"Actually," I clear my throat, "I finished my tour with them. I'm working in my old building, on a different floor, some other company."

"Oh yeah?" Zelda says. "Maybe I'll try and meet you for lunch. The Johnstons like me to get the kid out as much as possible."

"A nanny's work is never done," I tell her.

"Not until people start raising their own kids." Zelda picks up her bag and starts fishing through it. She pulls out her Muni pass. "How's twelve-thirty, downtown?"

"I would," I tell her. "But I don't know when they give me a lunch. It'd be hard to meet up."

"Yeah, yeah," she says with a frown. "You're getting sick of me."

"Not at all," I tell her. "Let's do it tomorrow, my treat."

"You've got yourself a date, Mr. Parrish."

Zelda and I go our separate ways at the Muni. I grab the M and she waits for the N. I don't have a job this week. I will take the train downtown, spend a few hours in the library emailing out my résumé, checking the want ads, and calling temp agencies. Then I will get back on the Muni, this time the N train, and go to Martha.

We have developed a routine since we started sleeping together. We'll spend two hours together, have sex, and then we will fight. If the fights get really heated, we'll have sex again. It's not a horrible way to spend an afternoon.

JB has sent me another email. He wants to meet up at yet another bar that I don't recognize by name. I have been dodging him for a few weeks, which isn't easy since we live in the same house. I think it would be suspect to keep avoiding him. Once I finish up my work at the library, I jump on a train and head to Martha's. When I get there, she is already crying.

"What's the matter?" I ask.

"Nothing," she tells me after taking a long moment to think.

"Are you sure?"

"Yeah, family stuff."

"I am sorry," I tell her and put my arm around her. I pull her close and hold her. She feels like home to me, but I don't tell her. We make our way to her bedroom, all the while kissing and fumbling with each other's clothes.

When she screams out, "Jesus Christ," in my ear, I think it's because I've done something awesome sex-wise. Even when she slaps my back and tells me to stop I don't understand. It's not until I hear Bobby's voice that I realize what has happened.

"Heavens," Bobby vamps.

"This isn't what it looks like," Martha says.

"It looks like hide the salami to me," Bobby teases.

"I can explain," I say while jumping out of bed. I'm naked. Bobby looks me up and down and winks at me. I look back to Martha, she didn't catch it.

"You can't say anything to JB," Martha says. She is about to cry. "Please promise me, Bobby. Promise me you won't say anything. Ethan, make him promise. He'll ruin everything."

"I will," I tell her. "I'll fix it." I put on my boxers, then grab Bobby by the arm and take him into the kitchen, and we go out to the fire escape.

"Naughty little boy," Bobby teases.

"Don't be cute."

"I can't help it," he says, pursing his lips. "I am as God made me."

"You're impossible to talk to," I scold him. "You know that, right?"

"Be nice, Ethan." Bobby crosses his arms over his chest and adjusts his posture. "I'd hate to think about what would happen if we weren't friends anymore."

"You have to promise to keep this secret," I say. I am doing my best serious voice, trying to convey the importance of the situation.

"I don't know." Bobby puts his hands on my shoulders and shakes his head, solemn-like. He considers my plea. "It's getting hard to keep all your sordid business quiet."

"I'll do anything you want."

"This sounds promising," Bobby smirks.

"You're not even attracted to me," I say.

"I know, but the power gets me off." Bobby grabs me between my legs and kisses me forcefully. I put up little resistance and then I kiss him back. Bobby and I have slept together a handful of times since I started seeing Martha. My heart feels like it could burst out of my chest and shoot off this fire escape.

"If you don't fight, it's not as hot," he tells me, his lips on mine.

"My God," Martha says. I push Bobby away and see her head poking out of the kitchen window.

"It's not what it looks like," I tell her, dizzy from the kiss. "Let me explain. Bobby, wait out here." I climb in through the window. When I look back at Bobby, he is smiling, really enjoying himself. I take Martha into the living room. She has gone completely white in the face, her mouth is agape.

"So what's up with all that stuff out there?" she asks.

"He just went nuts and kissed me."

"I don't believe that one bit," Martha says. She is quiet for a moment and then her eyes light up. "Oh my God, you fucked Bobby."

"That's crazy," I say and then hurry into the bedroom to get my clothes.

"I never thought you were the most macho guy in the world, but a full-blown homo?" Martha says. "Wow, I can't believe it."

"I'm not gay."

"Fucking Bobby is pretty gay."

"I can't talk to either of you," I say. "I've got to go downtown and meet your boyfriend. I'll try not to mention all the heterosexual sex I've been having with you."

"Don't tell JB anything," Martha says. "It'll fuck up your life as much as it will fuck up mine. Think about JB," she warns. "Think about Zelda. They deserve better than us." She continues to call after me even when I'm outside her apartment. "Don't ruin everything, you fucking homo."

JB

When I get off the train, my hands are shaking so much that I can't light my cigarette. I took too many of the one pill and not enough of the other. I see JB through the window of the bar. He is sitting in a booth. I finally get my cigarette lit and it tastes horrible. JB hasn't spotted me. I lean against the building opposite the bar and watch him. He is reading a copy of the *San Francisco Chronicle*, dressed in his best business clothes and sipping a pint of beer. I can't tell you the last time I cared enough to pick up a paper or put on anything more formal than a short-sleeved t-shirt over a long-sleeved t-shirt. I take a deep drag, cough, then flick my butt to the ground. This street smells funny to me.

"Hey, bud," JB says to me as I sit down across from him. "How do?"

"Not bad."

"You look like shit."

"Thanks."

"Everything okay?"

"I think I'm coming down with something." The waitress comes by and I order a drink. It is impossible for me to look JB in the eye. I sneak glances at his face but can't look any higher than his chin.

"I should just cut to the chase," JB says.

"You're seeing Martha," I interrupt him.

"You knew?"

"I had a pretty good idea."

"I'm sorry, man. I know I kind of went behind your back, but I really like this girl."

"Yeah, she's something." The waitress drops off my drink and I take a sip. The taste is off, maybe it's flat.

"I just figured since things were going so well between you and Zelda that I'd finally clear the air," JB says. "I also wanted to tell you that I'm moving out."

"Dude, you don't have to do that."

"No, it's not like that. Martha's pregnant." JB can't hold back his smile. "We're getting a place together and, you know, marriage pretty soon."

"I'm sorry, what?" I ask, but I heard him clearly. My shaky hand fumbles with my pint and I knock the glass over. "Shit, sorry."

"No worries," JB says, jumping out of his seat. He inspects his pants to see if I caught him. "Kind of a shock, huh?"

"Yeah, that's great, JB," I tell him while sloshing my spilt beer around with a handful of napkins. "I mean it, really great. Pregnant?" I keep going over the now-dry table with wet napkins. For a split second I consider telling him everything, telling him how his girlfriend and his best friend are awful, terrible people. But he looks so happy, like this is something he always wanted, and that surprises me. I didn't know that about him. "When did she tell you?"

"She hasn't yet." JB sits back down and leans over the table. "I found a pregnancy test in her bathroom."

"Are you serious?"

"It's not like I was snooping around, I had a bad nose bleed in the middle of the night. I didn't want to leave all my bloody tissues in the trash, so I emptied the can for her." JB is now whispering. "It fell out on the floor. You can't tell her. She'll think I was snooping."

"She doesn't know you know?"

"Not yet." JB leans back and runs his forearm across his brow. "I wanted to ask her to move in with me before she told me she was pregnant. You know, so she wouldn't think I was just doing it because of the baby." His thumbs are pounding out a rhythm on the table. "You really don't look so hot."

"Something's been going around the office."

"Which office is that?" JB's phone rings. "Shit, that's work."

"Take it," I tell him. I start to feel nauseous, and little beads of cold sweat blister at the surface of my skin. JB walks away from his table. I don't understand what he's saying. He is using his work voice, a voice I don't have.

"I'm sorry, I've got to get back," he says. "We cool?"

"Totally," I say.

"Thanks." JB smiles and taps out a final drumroll on the table. "Please keep this under wraps until I get a chance to talk to Martha."

"No problem." I wave goodbye to JB.

As soon as he is out of sight, I rush to the bathroom. My heart is racing and I can't catch my breath. I splash water on my face as if it will wash away all the sins of my world. I look in the mirror. My face is all scrunched up, and the water dribbling down my face looks like tears.

"Boo hoo," I say out loud. "Poor JB, boo hoo." And I say Martha's name and Zelda's name, and I think of that bastard growing in Martha's belly, and I say, "Boo hoo," for each one of them. I splash my face with water again and say my name and then boo hoo. I hurt my own feelings, but no real tears come. I dry my face, turn off the faucet, and then leave. I need to find Zelda. I need to be told it's okay.

Me

I want out of my head as I walk up Columbus Avenue. I catch sight of Zelda in the park. She's just where she said she would be. This is how good people act. They tell others that they will be at a certain place, at a certain time, because that's where they'll be. She has Peter in a stroller and is feeding him from a jar of baby food. She laughs when he waves his hands up and down, happy to be spoonfed such sweetness. She is good at taking care of babies.

"What are you doing here?" Zelda asks. She's genuinely happy to see me. Her emotions are always right at the surface.

"I was thinking about you," I tell her. "So I decided to stop by."

"Aren't you sweet?"

"Don't you know it?" I lean in and give her a kiss. It makes her blush. She is not used to me being so openly affectionate. "I need to tell you something."

"What is it, Ethan?"

"I want you to know that I love you."

"Don't be funny, Ethan," she tells me. "This isn't something to be funny about."

"I'm serious, Zelda. I love you. Do you love me?"

"Of course I do," she says, her eyes tearing up. "Of course I do."

"You make me happy." I put my arms around her and kiss her on top of her head. I take in a deep breath, my nose nestled in her hair. The way she smells makes me feel better. My heart slows to a bearable beat.

WHEN IT WAS GOOD

This was before everything went to shit, but right at the end of the really good part. The whole town smelled like campfire and it rained ash into your wine as we sat and talked over drinks in the courtyard of that Mexican place that sold tumblers full of tequila for more than the cost of the pants I wore. This is when you smiled at me and absentmindedly swirled your finger around the rim of your glass. I vaguely remember saying something that I only half believed, and you looked at me like I was a total asshole. We'd known each other for some time, so I was surprised you'd just stumbled onto the idea. To be perfectly honest, I thought you already knew. I watched as the spark in your eye was blown out by the breath of my voice, and I thought, *What a shame.* I really liked you. But this was before that, when it was good.

A SONG FOR ORPHANS

I t was Tuesday, Zoe Ketchum was a full month into the fall
semester of her freshman year, and she had never felt so
alone. She hadn't heard from her mother in more months
than she cared to count. She'd met people at school, but they
quickly faded into the background of her life. And then there
was Luke. She didn't even know his phone number, hadn't ever
called him before. She almost couldn't believe it. Her father, on

the other hand, wouldn't stop calling. It had become harder and harder for Zoe to ignore him. This idea that maybe he wasn't totally responsible for her mother's longstanding absence gained traction in her mind.

Zoe looked up from her textbook. The boy with the greasy dark hair sitting across from her was picking his nose, knuckle deep, as they say. She cleared her throat. The boy reacted and quickly hid his hand under the table. Zoe continued to look at him for a moment. His gaze remained locked on his textbook as his face reddened. Her attention turned from the boy to the Student Center's muted television. It was set on a news station. She read the ticker at the bottom of the screen: Walter Leeds had been killed. Zoe vaguely recognized the name but couldn't place it. She pulled her phone from her bag and checked the time. She had two missed calls from her father, both from the night before. Zoe started to return his call but hung up. She didn't want to fight with him anymore. She was tired of the arguing, tired of the back-and-forth yelling. It was all nonsense at this point, yard dogs barking at each other from opposite sides of the fence. Blow-outs, that's what she called their fights. There would be this tremendous pressure building between her and her father and then boom, a blow-out.

"You can't fool me," Zoe yelled at her father. This was back in those desperate late summer days, just weeks before she would leave for school. Her powerful scream echoed in the wide hallway of their beachfront house. This was a blow-out for the ages. She had just been told that her mother would not be coming back to the States for Thanksgiving, as promised. Zoe slammed the door to her room as her father moved closer.

"I'm not trying to fool you," Mortimer spoke through the door. "You have to know, I don't want to keep you two apart."

"I don't believe you," Zoe answered. "You lie, like all the time. And you're not just a liar; you're like a total asshole, too."

"That's enough," Mortimer said firmly.

Zoe watched the already locked doorknob jiggle. Her father's frustration delighted her. The door bowed as Mortimer leaned into it and then shuddered when he gave it a good kick. "You don't call me that, do you understand me?"

"I'll call you anything I like," Zoe said. "Mom's gone and it's your fault."

"I'm not doing this anymore," Mortimer replied, much quieter this time. "We'll talk about this in the morning, when you're calm." His footsteps clapped against the hardwood floor in the hallway; the sound faded until going silent on the soft carpet of his bedroom.

Zoe lay in bed, on top of the sheets with her fists clenched and muscles constricted. She tried to relax by conjuring up thoughts that didn't involve smashing or breaking her father's face. Eventually, her mind settled, her heart beat slowed and her arms hung loose by her side. Finally, she fell asleep.

The quick repeated ringing of the doorbell pulled Zoe awake. The fist-pounded banging that followed brought her to her feet. She looked at the clock. It was well into the morning hours. Zoe stuck her head into the hallway and saw her father emerge from his room.

"Get back in your room," Mortimer commanded, in a low, forceful tone. Zoe, stunned by his firmness, complied quickly. Thinking better of her initial reaction, she opened the door a crack and gazed out. Mortimer flipped the upstairs light switch and illuminated the foyer. The ruckus at the front door stopped. Zoe watched as Mortimer looked over the second-floor railing cautiously, and then swiftly moved down the stairs. Zoe, feeling bold, opened her door farther and tiptoed down the hall. With her body close to the wall, she crouched down and snuck a look through the first spindle of banister.

Mortimer had flipped the porch lights on and was at the peephole. He moved his hand towards the deadbolt and started to turn it. Mortimer jumped back just before the door shook with a violent thud. There was a faint sound of broken glass followed by moaning. Mortimer got up on his tiptoes and tried to get a better angle on the peephole. He looked over his shoulder and caught sight of his Zoe standing at the top of the stairs.

"Call the cops," Mortimer called up to his daughter. His words were rushed and he sounded a bit out of breath.

"Please," a man's voice came from the open mail slot which sat in the middle of the door. "Don't call the cops, I'm leaving."

"Luke?" Mortimer asked. He crouched down to get level with the mail slot.

"No," the man answered. "It's not me." The brass of the mail slot smacked closed.

"Zoe," Mortimer said. "I'm going to open the door. If he steps one foot into this house, lock yourself in your room and wait for the police." Mortimer pulled an umbrella from the stand next to the door and held it as weapon. He flipped the lock on the dead bolt and pulled the door open as if to surprise. Luke was unconscious. The frequently intoxicated fireman, who lived in the tiny soapbox house behind the Ketchum's three-story mansion, had long been suspected of tampering with the Ketchum's house. There were frequent late-night ring and runs, human feces in flaming bags on the doorstep, and egg splattered on their cars.

"Is he dead?" Zoe asked.

"No," Mortimer replied and gave Luke a nudge with his foot. "He's breathing."

The police arrived and collected Luke off the front porch. They deposited him face down in the back of their car. The attending officers took him to the municipal jail for a night in the drunk tank. Mortimer watched and waited for the police to pull away before bolting the door and going bed.

"What's that?" Zoe asked. Her eyes lit up as she slid into her seat at the breakfast table. There was a letter with Luke's name on it sitting near Mortimer.

"I have some business to sort out with our neighbor. I think a letter might be the best way to handle it." Mortimer scanned the morning paper. A cut grapefruit sprinkled with Splenda sat ignored in front of him. "Less awkward," he added.

"I heard Luke's father split town after you gave him the check for this lot." Zoe grabbed the rectangular glass vase in the center of the table and pulled it to her place setting. She put her nose into the fresh lilies and inhaled deeply.

"That's just gossip."

"Left Luke without a nickel and a dying mother to care for," she continued from behind the flowers. "That's sad. What is he twenty-five and already no family left?"

"Even if that's true," Mortimer folded his paper down in order to make eye contact with Zoe, who was still partially hidden by the lilies, "it's really none of our business."

"Dad, if you cheated on Mom, does that mean you will cheat on everyone you marry?" she asked. "I saw this thing on *Oprah* about how cheaters always cheat."

"Please," Mortimer said softly, "just have some breakfast, okay?"

"I'm not eating today," Zoe said. "I feel fat."

"You're hardly over a hundred pounds. You need to eat."

"Ew," Zoe grimaced. "Don't talk about my weight."

"You don't need to lose any, that's all," Mortimer offered.

"I'll take this over to Luke." Zoe put her wavy blond hair into a ponytail, then grabbed the letter off the table. Mortimer called out a protest as she neared the door, but it was ignored.

As Zoe walked down the dune, she thought about Luke. She liked the way he'd scared Mortimer that night. It made her want to get close to him. Zoe knocked on the door and found his house empty. She took a seat on his porch swing with the letter in her lap. Before long, Zoe heard stumbling sounds along the walkway beside the house. She heard the squeaky valve of the hose faucet turn, followed by the sloppy sound of rushed water. There was a loud moan followed by a few mumbled calls to a God with many names. "Jesus Christ, Dear Lord, Fhaaaghuk me," she heard him pray. Luke appeared on the porch, dripping wet with his shirt hanging out of his back pocket.

"This is from my Dad," she told him, holding the envelope out.

"What is that?" Luke turned his head and coughed before reaching for the letter. "Like a summons or something?"

"Just a letter," she said. "My dad doesn't want it to be weird."

"Is that a fact?" Luke grabbed the letter from her and opened it up. He began reading it, then stopped and looked at Zoe. "Well, thanks. You can run along now."

"Aren't you going to ask me in for a drink?" Zoe asked.

"Where are my manners?" Luke said. He propped open the screen, then kicked open the front door, holding it for her. Zoe brushed up against him as she entered the house. He had left all the windows open all night, but the place smelled of stale beer and cigarette smoke. The house felt damp with sea air. She took a few steps towards the middle of the room and then just stood there. The ill-fitted screen door slammed against the frame and then bounced open. The hairs on back of her neck went on end.

"What do you drink?" Luke was right behind her. She turned and kissed him.

"Listen," Luke took a step back. "What's your name?"

"Zoe."

"Zoe." Luke had his hands on her shoulders with his arms fully extended. "I think you better get going."

"Don't be such a faggot," Zoe said.

"You're quite a charmer, princess." Luke chuckled. "Still want that drink?"

"I wasn't really interested in the drink."

"If you caught me at the right time, maybe." Luke walked into his kitchen, pulled a dirty glass from the sink, and filled it with bourbon. "But being fresh from county and all, I'm thinking to myself, maybe shacking up with jailbait isn't the best way to get right with God."

"I'm not so young."

"Whatever, it doesn't matter." Luke took a pull from his drink. "You're trouble and I got my week's worth of that last night."

"You're lame." Zoe walked passed Luke and out the door. "Come see me when you grow a set." As she walked up the dune, her scrunched angry face faded. A smile emerged. Zoe entered the house. Her father was still sitting at the kitchen table reading his paper.

"Hey Daddy," Zoe greeted her father sweetly. She walked toward him with a smile on her face. He was very much like a dog, she thought. It didn't matter what she said to him as long as her tone sounded pleasant. "I gave Luke the letter."

"Thanks, honey."

If he had big floppy ears, they would have perked up now.

"I don't like you fraternizing with him." Mortimer folded the paper in half. "He's a troubled young man."

"I also gave him a blowjob," she said.

"Zoe," Mortimer snapped.

"He said thanks." Zoe smiled at her reddening father; he looked as if he was about to stroke out. She turned and happily skipped out of the room. As she galloped up the stairs, Zoe heard the violent screech of her father's metal chair against the marble kitchen floor. Mortimer was down the hallway and out the front door in an angry flash. Zoe was already on the second-floor balcony by the time Mortimer had left the house. She plopped herself in a lounge chair and gripped the pillow with both hands, anxious for the show. An evil smile contorted her face as she watched him storm down the dune.

Mortimer stepped onto Luke's front porch, then disappeared under the roof. She heard her father angrily banging on the screen door. It went quiet for a moment before the muffled sounds of heated words rose to her ears. She couldn't make out what they were saying—the noise registered as nothing more than unintelligible grunts. Zoe rolled off the lounge chair and tried to get a better vantage. She was on the treated wood of the deck now, cheek to the floor, straining to see what was happening below. Mortimer appeared. He took long strides back up the dune, talking to himself the whole way, gesturing conductor-like with his arms. Luke came out a moment later. He stopped his charge after a few feet. Luke had a hand over his right eye. His other hand held the phone to his ear.

Zoe almost burst into laughter. She rolled over onto her back holding her stomach. God, she wished her mom was here to see it; she'd love it. But where was her mom? Somewhere in Europe, maybe? The last postcard had a picture of the Eiffel Tower and bore the water stain of a carelessly placed rock's glass. But that card was months old by now. Zoe rolled over on her side and pulled her knees into her chest. She worried about other things sometimes. She worried that something was wrong with her, something innate that made her forgettable. Zoe wondered what it felt like to be totally forgotten. She wondered if it felt anything like the way she felt right now.

The police arrived at the Ketchum house promptly. Zoe watched, from the front porch, as the police cuffed her father and then placed him in the back of their vehicle. She glanced down the dune to Luke. He was standing on his front porch with a drink in his hand. Luke raised the glass to Zoe, and then placed the drink on his right eye. He raised his free hand and wagged *no-no* with his finger. She looked back to her father, seething in the back of the patrol car, and waved to him. Then she turned back to Luke and blew him a kiss.

Feeling victorious, with the blood pumping strongly in her veins, Zoe decided to hit the gym. She pulled a mat from the wall and laid it out on the weight-room floor. As she stretched, she thought about Luke. She thought about walking down the dune and having a drink with him, but it seemed like a waste without Mortimer around to see it. Zoe wanted her father to hear her down there, on Luke's porch. She'd laugh just loud enough for Mortimer to hear. He'd get so mad. The phone rang. Annoyed, she exhaled before standing up from the mat. Zoe walked over to the phone and checked the number on the caller ID. It was the police department.

"Zoe," Mortimer's voice came from the answering machine. "I need you to come down here with my credit card and bail me out." The speaker went quiet except for the hiss of a bad connection. "Please," Mortimer added. Zoe hit the erase button when the message ended.

The next morning Zoe refolded the clothes on her bed so she could fit them all in her luggage. She heard the sound of a car door slamming. She glanced out of her window and watched her father talk to the cab driver through the passenger-side window. Mortimer ran into the house, presumably to grab some money. Zoe went back to packing. School didn't start for a few weeks, but she'd had it with this house. Mortimer slammed the front door.

"Zoe," Mortimer said. "Get down here."

She threw her smaller bag over her shoulder and picked her suitcase up. Zoe moved down the staircase, her eyes locked on her father. She walked right up to him and then dropped her bags on the marble floor.

"Where do you think you're going?" Mortimer asked.

"I'm leaving," Zoe answered, "for school."

"Did you get my message?"

"Yup."

"You're an ungrateful little shit."

"And you're a joke of a man," Zoe replied. "You ran mom off, and I don't have to stay here anymore either."

"Your mother left both of us."

"Because you cheated on her," she said.

"Your mother gave you up," Mortimer said. "She told her lawyer to trade custody of you for more money."

"You're so pathetic," Zoe said. She felt short of breath, her voice went to a whisper. "I hate you." She picked her bags up and walked out the door. "I'm taking a car, call it stolen if you want."

Mortimer started calling Zoe every day, leaving apologetic messages. He told her he felt horrible for how he spoke to her. He pleaded with her voicemail day in and day out. When that didn't work, he tried to be stern. And after realizing neither tone got his daughter on the phone, he'd leave long messages full of trivial details. He told her about his commute from the Jersey shore to his Manhattan office. Mortimer had started taking a helicopter to work. A New York television host from a twenty-four-hour news station had moved next door; since they worked in the same building, he offered Mortimer a seat in the aircraft. Mortimer told her voicemail that everything was less congested, now that all the renters had gone home. He told her how someone started drilling holes in the dingy that was docked with their yacht, sinking it at least once a week. Sometimes he would forgo work to stay home and patch the thing up. He'd often find it sunk again the next day. Mortimer implied that it might be Luke. Zoe knew it couldn't possibly be anyone else. Over all, it was an uneventful time, and he missed her more and more as each day passed.

As Zoe floated between Tuesday's morning and afternoon classes, she thought about Walter Leeds. He was back on the television. She walked over to the screen and turned up the sound. He was the host of a show called *If It's News, It's Leeds*, and he lived in the same beach town as she did. Walter Leeds, the news anchor reported, had been killed in a helicopter crash along with four others.

Details were sketchy. Zoe shook her head as if she had just been abruptly pulled from sleep. The mystery was gone, the name was understood. She ran back to her room, tore it apart, hunting for her car keys. She couldn't remember where she'd left them. The car had just been sitting there, idle in the parking garage for weeks. She just needed to get home. Keys, keys, keys, where are those keys goddamn keys? It was all she could think.

Zoe had no memory of the three-hour drive home. She had no memory of pulling up in the driveway or even putting her key in the front-door lock or turning the knob. It was as if she had just appeared in her kitchen. And now that she was home, there was more uneasiness, more fog, and more fear. The flowers at the center of the table seemed slightly wilted to her eye, the air breathed stale. The house felt empty, but not in the way that there's simply nobody home. It felt empty in the way the full moon felt empty when she looked up to it from the beach on a cloudless night. Nothing lived up there, and that's how her father's house felt. She corrected her posture so she could stand strong, and be strong, but the room started to spin. She weakly touched her forehead with a shaking hand. Zoe sat down on the floor before the collapse.

··•··

Two weeks went by in a gray and black blur of extended family, lawyers, priests, and total strangers. Tin trays of food occupied every possible bit of counter space in the kitchen. It would be impossible for Zoe to go through the rest of her life without smelling deli meats or baked Ziti and not think about death. The house was quiet for the first time since the funeral. Zoe walked onto the back deck and took in a deep noseful of salty ocean air. She caught sight of Luke sitting on his back porch sipping on a drink.

"Hey," Zoe called to Luke as she walked down the dune towards his porch.

"Hey," Luke called back.

"How've you been?"

"Not bad," Luke shrugged. "You?"

"I don't know." Zoe sat down next to him on his porch swing. "Terrible. Insane, maybe?"

"Yeah." Luke took a sip of iced tea. He held his glass up to Zoe. "Do you want some? I've got a jug inside."

"Sure," Zoe answered. She slid her feet back and forth over the sand that had piled up on the porch. "I heard you quit drinking."

"Who told you that?" Luke asked as he stood up.

"Ralph."

"From the station?"

"That's right."

"Didn't realize you two knew each other," Luke said before walking into his house. The rusty screen door screeched before banging into the frame of the house.

"We don't," Zoe said. "I stopped by looking for you."

"Is that so?"

"He said you took off right before the crash," Zoe said. She started making circles in the sand with her feet.

"Yeah, that's right." Luke emerged from the house. The metal once again creaked. He handed her the glass of iced tea and leaned against the porch post.

"Where'd you go?" Zoe looked at the ice as it continued to swirl around from having the sugar stirred in and then took a sip.

"This place a few hours south," Luke answered. "They helped me with the drinking."

"It's funny," Zoe said softly. "I remember thinking that maybe my dad was okay, you know? Maybe you sank his boat, and he didn't go into work that day."

"I'd like that," Luke said softly. "He was on my list, for the amends."

"I know you didn't like my dad."

"Truth is, I didn't know him," Luke admitted. "I was just mad, and not at him neither. Just mad and dumb and drunk."

"It's okay." Zoe let out a sad chuckle. "I didn't treat him too good myself."

"Yeah, well, it's not your fault," he said. "You're a fucked-up kid and all. But still, it's not on you." Luke gave Zoe an awkward smile, then took a long sip of his drink. He tilted his head back until there was no liquid left and the ice cubes rushed to his face.

"I know it, I guess," Zoe said. "But it feels like my fault. It feels like this is punishment." She sniffled a bit before continuing. "Anyway, thanks for coming to the funeral. That took some guts, I think. My own mother didn't even come."

Zoe hung her head after admitting this to Luke. She didn't want to cry, sitting there on his porch swing, drinking iced tea. But she didn't want to fight it either. Luke, with some hesitation, moved towards her and took a seat beside her. She wrapped her arms around him and buried her face in his chest. They stayed like that for awhile.

THE GARY GAME

Since the Old Boy caught me smoking pot, he's been a huge pain in my ass. As I walk back from communion, I enjoy one of the few moments he isn't directly over my shoulder. In his absence I count the pews. I count how many rows make up the church, from altar to exit. There are thirty-six this week, same as last week.

Mary Lou Akimbo and her family sit six rows down on the opposite side of the church. Me and Mary Lou did it a month ago,

and I can't stop thinking about when we're going to do it again.
I can't go more than five minutes without getting a boner. It's
gotten so bad that I have to bring the mass book with me when
I walk to communion. I should really carry one with me at all
times. I watch Mary Lou when she takes the host from the priest.
She looks over her shoulder as she genuflects and catches my eye.
I want her so bad, but I can't see her until I'm off punishment. The
Old Boy says that's not going to happen until I've earned his trust
back. Whatever that means.

There's a problem—they ran short of mass books. I have to
fold my hands over my inappropriate bulge as I shuffle down
the aisle. My mother follows close behind me. The Old Boy never
goes with us. I've always wanted to ask him why he doesn't
take communion, but I don't. I'm afraid he'll say he suffers from
the same affliction that plagues me, constant and unrelenting
erections. I've decided to keep my curiosity to myself.

Father Funt offers me his hand as I exit the church. He smiles
and says, "God be with you."

"That's a really nice crucifix on your frock," I tell him. He
smiles at me and it is a warm smile and it makes me feel good.
"It's probably way nicer then the one Jesus was nailed to," I add.
His smile fades. When we get to the car, far from Father Funt's
eyesight, the Old Boy slaps me over the back of the head.

"How many times do I have to tell you?" The Old Boy pinches
the arch of his nose with his thumb and forefinger and sighs.
"Enough with that, okay?"

As the Old Boy takes the driver's seat of the car, it gives under
his girth. He is a wad of a man. The Old Boy's thick forearms and
swollen hands are reminders of all his years slinging bags of
cement, piles of wood and heavy rental equipment off the back of
trucks. I have no such definition. More than one family member
has told me that I look more like the mailman than my father.
The Old Boy turns to me and starts to speak but stops himself. He
faces forward and turns on the car. I don't say anything. Mom lets
out the tiniest laugh and tries to cover by saying "Bless me," as if
she sneezed.

I spend the rest of Sunday sitting in the local bar next to my father. He jokes with whoever's in earshot and bets on games with anyone who will take his action. He doesn't have as many friends as he used to. The Old Boy used to run with a great big crowd. Everyone around me was an uncle or an aunt but rarely blood relation. That all changed after he sold the store. After the layoffs, my aunts and uncles didn't come around as much, then not at all. The Old Boy's construction-supply company is now just a parking lot, and somehow that bothers him, like it makes the selling of his shop and the end of those friendships that much more meaningless. I once heard him talking to his brother on the phone about it. He said, "Fuck 'em. Home Depot was gonna put us out of business anyway. I have my own family to look out for." As it starts to get dark out, the Old Boy settles up his bets.

"What if I just give you Gary and we call it even," the Old Boy tells the guy next to him. "How about it, Ethan?" He nudges me. "Let's keep the money and give him Gary."

"I don't think Gary would mind," I say into my soft drink. Gary is the family dog, but sometimes we're not actually talking about him.

Back at home, Sunday dinner gets under way. Mom is in the kitchen on pasta and salad. She picks up Gary and sits him on a barstool, pours a glass of wine and starts talking. We all talk to Gary in passing, but Mom actually gets conversation out of him.

"Of course, I think it's ridiculous, but what am I supposed to do?" she says. The slight cosmopolitan version of my mother, the one that enchants crowds at social gatherings, is gone. Her thick South Jersey accent comes out when she talks with Gary. I can't see her from where I'm sitting, but I know her hand is up in front of her face with her thumb, middle and index fingers all touching. "Well, you know what?" Her wide Sicilian nose, a mirror image of my own, is flaring. "Someday I just might do that, Gary. And then where would they be?" She takes a sip of wine and says, "Exactly."

I'm in the den watching TV. The Old Boy is out back poking at steaks on the grill. I don't do anything to help prepare dinner, mostly because I really don't like doing things that would increase my chances of talking to either one of them. I spend the dinner fearing they'll speak to me. Any moment they could jump down my throat and try to converse with me or ask me how things in my life "are going." It's sick.

Mom is a quick-draw artist with the remote. Any sound, be it a throat clear, clang of silverware, or dog fart, and she hits mute. Gary barks for food and Mom pounces. We all stop chewing and look around the table like we're in some hammy Agatha Christie novel. I immediately start sweating. What do they know? What have they found hidden in my room? Alcohol? Maybe the last of my pot? My parents remain cool, waiting for me to crack. The pressure becomes too much and I break. "I need new pants," I blurt out almost in tears. "These are getting too tight."

"Alright," the Old Boy says before getting up from the table. He opens the back door, and Gary goes happily traipsing out into the night. "Get some exercise, Gary. You're a fat dog." He sits back down and we finish the meal in silence. I clean my plate in the sink, then rush upstairs and call Mary Lou.

"Hey," I say into the phone. "How's my girl?"

"Oh, hi," Mary Lou replies. She sounds kind of annoyed to hear from me. This is strange because since we did it she's been really interested in everything I've had to say. "So I heard a song on the radio today. It sounded a lot like *Untitled love poem number 8*. Pretty weird, huh?" she asks.

Mary Lou was under the impression that I was a poet. I sometimes read things like *Untitled love poem number 8* to her over the phone at night. Mostly the poems were song lyrics I'd copied down and passed off as my own. I tried to stick to obscure bands, but it seems one broke free from college radio.

"We're over. And by the way, you're a bad kisser," she says and then hangs up.

I call her back at least a dozen times. With each phone call I become more desperate. Finally, I just flat out tell Mary Lou that I love her. I get this really weird feeling all over. "Please," I beg.

Mary Lou lets out a breathy laugh and hangs up.

Everyone at school knows what happened. Apparently, Mary Lou had a few of her friends over that night. They listened to my obsessive calls, and I've heard they even made a recording. I told my friends that the break-up really upset me, and I didn't want any of them going out with her. They told me, "No problem," but kind of laughed as they said it. I keep calling Mary Lou every night, but she always seems to be on the phone with someone else. I ask her who it is, and she just says some guy.

I'm feeling real shitty lately. Everyone at school knows I got dumped. What's even worse, I heard Mary Lou and Jim Williams did it. I think I could take getting dumped, but getting dumped and knowing she's sleeping with that douche is more than I can take.

Yesterday walking back from the lunchroom, I heard my voice coming from a group of girls sitting in a circle. The quality of the recording was impressively clear. You could even hear me sniffling. When the girls saw me passing, they shut off the recording. They were barely able to hold back their giggles as I passed.

Now I really want to kill myself. The thing is I can't say that I'm all that comfortable with the permanence of suicide. And although every day feels like the worst day, today seems especially bad. Mary Lou just walked by me in the hallway and didn't even make eye contact. Last night I called her and found out her number had been changed.

Everything just totally sucks, and I can't stop reading *The Catcher in the Rye*. To tell the truth, I'm not really reading the book. I only read certain parts. But I do like carrying it around with me. It gives me some kind of arty sensitive look. It was banned from school. Plus, it helps with boner camouflage.

Janice Heffelfinger crouches down in front of my desk during study hall and starts talking. I can see right down her blouse. Janice says something about meeting her on the baseball field after class, I think. It's very tough to concentrate when those things are on display like that. We're talking an eyeful here.

Somehow it occurs to me that Janice is playing the messenger. This could be the news I've been waiting for. Maybe Mary Lou has had a change of heart. The next few minutes pass like hours; finally, the bell rings. I've started reading the part where Holden is whining about something again. He's such a crybaby touchhole. It makes me thank God for pot, because without it I'd probably be just as bad.

Janice is sitting in the dugout waving me over. I'm a little upset that Mary Lou didn't come herself. Still, any news is good news. I ask her what's going on. Janice tells me that she has liked me for a long time. She says she was going to tell me, but when I started dating Mary Lou, she thought she'd missed her chance.

"I'm not going to let that happen again," she says, then leans in to kiss me. We make out for a while, and when we're done, I feel much better about myself. It's amazing how getting a handjob in a baseball dugout can change your perspective on life.

Now that Janice and I are dating, Mary Lou calls me all the time. She tells me that the rumors about Jim Williams are lies, and if I believe them, I never really loved her. I'm not really sure what to make of all this. I did lie to her in the first place, but she made me feel horrible after the fact. Maybe that's how it is supposed to work. I think Mary Lou knows more about relationships than I do, and it might be a good idea if I follow her lead. Then again, I kind of get the idea that she might be talking to me just because I'm with Janice and that if I was still pathetic and alone, she wouldn't be calling me.

On my way to math class, Mary Lou stops me. She looks all serious and pained. Mary Lou apologizes for being so mean after we broke up and says it was all an act. I don't really understand what she means, but I have this feeling that what she just said makes everything okay.

"I'm so sorry," she says. It looks like she is hurting when she talks. "Let's get back together. I promise I'll be good and make everything right."

Part of me wants to accept her. I really liked Mary Lou when we were dating and there was all the sex stuff. And I said I loved her, too. But if I accept, that means I would probably hurt Janice, and she doesn't deserve such shoddy treatment. Janice recently started incorporating lotion into her handjobs. It's a nice touch.

"Well?" Mary Lou asks all impatient and kind of rude. Jim Williams walks by us. I catch him giving her an "I totally nailed you" wink. "Are we back together or not?"

"Did you have sex with him?"

"ETHAN!" Mary Lou stamps her foot. "How dare you."

"I'm sorry." I'm finding out that I'm really bad at confrontations. "But did you?"

"Does it matter?" she asks.

"I think it might."

"Did you and Janice do it?"

"I'm not sure if I should talk to you about this."

"If you can't confide in me, then I don't know if I want to be with you," Mary Lou says and turns away from me.

"Wait, don't leave like this."

She stops in the hallway, and even though she's not looking at me, I can tell she's mad. I don't like it when people are mad at me. "It doesn't have to be like, you know…" I trail off as I approach her. She turns to me, and before I know what's happening, we're kissing. It feels all wrong and really good at the same time. Then I hear Janice screaming at me from the other end of the hall.

"Jerkoff!" The words grab me by the root of my backbone and spin me around. "We're through."

"Wait, please listen." I catch sight of Janice's crimson-red face and can't come up with anymore words. She covers her face and runs around the corner, and before she's out of earshot, I hear her break into tears. I'm such a shit.

"You know," Mary Lou says, "you were a lot more attractive ten minutes ago." She turns away and leaves me standing alone in the hall.

"I'm worried about Gary," my mother says. "He's been moping around here more than usual."

Somehow my parents have gotten it in their heads that I'm suicidal. We're in the kitchen, and she is putting together a salad. She looks concerned. I feel responsible for this worry, and it makes me sad. My mom turns to my father and asks, "Do you think Gary is okay?"

I open the fridge and look for something to drink. The Old Boy tousles my hair as he walks by. He doesn't answer my mother.

"Doesn't Gary look unusually unhappy these days?" Mom asks, a little more insistent.

"Of course, he does," I say with my head in the fridge. "Gary's a teenager. He's supposed to be depressed."

COUNTY LINE

Billy catches sight of a trooper, and something occurs to him: he shouldn't have had all those boilermakers. He takes his foot off the gas and looks at the speedometer, thirty-seven in a twenty-five. On its own, it's not enough to turn a head. If he stole a Lexus, he'd be fine. If it wasn't two-thirty in the morning, there wouldn't be a problem. But it is, and Billy just stole a '32 Ford with a Road Runner engine, not the most inconspicuous car on the road. As the trooper passes, Billy taps on the brakes and paints the road behind him in red light. The trooper flips on his siren and swings around. Only the cop doesn't make it. He's a rookie. He fumbles into a three-point turn. Billy kills the headlights, fingers the Hurst, and it's monkey down. He's a half mile gone before the cop's up to speed. The hill swallows the Ford from sight, and Billy takes a quick right onto the unmarked utility road that crosses Barrett's farm. It's all he needs to disappear. The tree line behind Billy lights up red with the trooper's bubble lights. The cop speeds by the dirt road without a clue.

Road rocks scratch against the car. That'll cost Billy a few bucks. An unassembled, '32 Ford, three-window frame, runs anywhere between ten and fifteen grand. Not bad. Add anywhere from forty to sixty grand for the engine. It's a 440-ci engine with three two-barrel carbs and a Hemi. Add up the man hours that went into it, the leather seats, that Hurst. You'd never see this thing on the market for less than ninety grand. If he makes it to the shop, they'll give him two thousand for the whole thing.

Billy skulks through the suburban neighborhoods that sit on the Mercer County line. The route is solid. He's done it plenty of times before. Once he gets to the garage in Chester, the whole exchange won't take more than twenty minutes. The Ford'll be on a slow boat heading for Antwerp within twenty-four hours.

Billy sits idle at the stop sign on the corner of Kingsley Avenue and Bluebird Street a little too long. He's still a bit sloppy from those boilermakers. He should just go, but instead he pulls the car over. Billy kills the engine. His kid lives in the big yellow house on the corner, the one with all the leaves in the yard. Billy sees his boy's swing set peeking over the backyard fence. The boy lives with his mother and his grandparents. It's a pretty nice house.

Billy hasn't been much of a father to the boy. Rebecca was sixteen when he got her pregnant. They were at a party where Billy's girlfriend ran off with some other guy. Billy found Rebecca in a back room listening to music and smoking a joint. She named their son Peter. For a time she thought they should be together for the baby. Billy gave it a try.

There is a light on downstairs, probably Rebecca's dad. He'd fall asleep in front of the TV a lot. He owns the BMW dealership on Route One. The old man gave Billy a job, told him it was a family business and he could be part of it. It didn't sound like a bad deal. Billy learned a lot about cars in the short time he worked there. They taught him things in the garage. They taught him how to deal with alarms, locks, engines and ignitions.

Billy didn't see it at first, but the old man never thought he was good enough for his daughter. About a month into the new job, some cars went missing. This guy in the garage says to the police, he says, "This new kid kept asking how to turn off car alarms and such." He says, "I taught him stuff, you know. Stuff that we need to know in the garage, stuff that could help someone boost a car." There was talk of a case against Billy, charges being pressed. The old man, the white knight that he was, he said he'd take care of it *if* Billy stayed out of Rebecca's life and away from the kid. He'd even give Billy some money. Billy agreed, didn't even take a minute to think it over. The old man acted like he was doing Billy a huge favor. The old man got what he wanted, and Billy learned a little bit about how things work.

When Billy thinks about it, he thinks he's not such a bad guy. There are people in this world who like him; there's not many of them, but they're out there. But sitting across from his boy's house, Billy feels the badness inside him. Peter's four now, and Billy hasn't seen him in two years. The old man pushed him around and he folded. The old man was smarter and tougher. That nags at him.

Boilermakers will turn on you, he thinks as he runs his hands through his thick, white-blond, product-filled hair. The wind picks up and carries bunches of leaves off the lawn. Billy turns the car on and knocks the Hurst into gear. He eases his right foot to the floor, takes off his seatbelt and releases the clutch. Billy's at the helm of a wrecking machine. The wheels scream bloody murder as he works the clutch and the gas. He lets her rip. There's a cloud of white smoke hanging like a beehive behind the car. Sparks fly when he hits the curb. The Ford scatters leaves like boat wake as he cuts through the front yard. Billy thinks about the look on the old man's face as he drives through the bushes that border the house. *Daddy's home.*

THINGS YOU WOULD KNOW ABOUT PAUL IF YOU WERE HIS FRIEND

My friend Paul lives in a mansion. It's not his mansion. He's just watching it for a friend. The other night I went over to visit Paul in his mansion. I knocked on the door…nothing. I rang the bell and received no answer. It's hard to hear the door if you are way back in the TV room of Paul's mansion. I called his cell phone: no answer again. The walls of the house are so thick that it hinders the reception. I was able to get him on the house line and beckoned him to the front door.

Paul hadn't shaved in a few days and smelled like scotch. This was part of his getting-ready-for-summer diet: scotch, Marlboro Mediums, and SlimFast. I asked him how work was going, and he said he didn't like his job and wanted to quit (part of the reason he hadn't shaved). I told him he'd most likely get fired if that's how he dressed for work.

Paul likes plaid and patchwork preppie clothing. Often he will rummage through old-clothes boxes in the mansion for outfits to wear to work. During this particular visit, Paul was wearing blue corduroys with seagulls stitched up and down the pant legs, a pink button-down, a scarf, a tweed blazer, and aviator sunglasses. These are the kind of clothes Paul likes to wear when watching TV alone on a Tuesday night.

On Sunday, Kelly came home from the city and invited us over to Paul's mansion for a barbeque. Kelly and Paul are super-good friends. In fact, her parents own Paul's mansion. She lives in Manhattan, and her parents spend most of their time in Florida. When Kelly's parents come back to Princeton, he moves back in with his mother. This house is also a mansion, and Paul lives on the third floor. His mother is a detective sergeant in the prosecutor's office and carries a gun.

Sometimes "Johns" will pick up hookers in Trenton and look for a place to do their business. Paul's mom's house is in a neighborhood by the park where the hookers hang out. The "Johns" often end up parking their cars in front of her place. Paul's mom stays on the lookout for such shady dealings. If she sees a strange car parked in front of her house, she will go out to the car with her badge and gun. Usually this happens late at night, so when she knocks on the window, she is in her bathrobe. She never arrests them. She just tells the girls never to bring men back to her house again. So consider yourself warned, if you're picking up hookers in Trenton. Don't stop in front of Paul's mom's house for a tug.

My girlfriend Daphne and I arrived at Kelly's BBQ in Paul's mansion around 6:00 p.m. We brought hamburgers and hotdogs.

Kelly made Caesar-salad dressing from scratch. Paul seasoned
the hamburgers with freshly pressed garlic, Worcestershire
sauce, and spices. Daphne made kabobs with shrimp and scallops,
and I cut up zucchini and eggplant to be grilled. When we were
cooking the hamburgers, Paul told me how much he hated his job
and his piece-of-shit car. Paul drives a 1982 Toyota Tercel stick-
shift hatchback most of the year. He told me he couldn't wait
for the summer. In the summer, Paul lives at the Jersey Shore.
He rents a house with his friends. They all spend their weekends
there, but Paul makes it his home and lives there all week. The
commute won't bother him, because he will take his BMW out
from storage in his mom's garage and drive that all summer.
Everyone at the shore house says Paul has a seasonal disorder
because he is so miserable most the year and so happy during the
summer. Paul's also happier in the summer because he makes out
with college girls.

While almost in his thirties and sometimes living with his
mother, Paul still gets college girls. And not regular college girls,
either. Paul gets the kind of college girls you couldn't get when
you were in college. Hell, Paul couldn't get these girls when he
was in college. In fact, if you are in college now and have a crush
on some unattainable girl, Paul probably made out with her.
Strange, I know. But fret not. Paul's seasonal disorder makes
it impossible for him to keep a relationship for more than
three months. Once Labor Day passes, his mood goes sour. Last
summer he broke up with his girlfriend over email. He said he felt
suffocated and needed more space. She was taking a semester
abroad at the time. That's about all I can tell you about Paul.

SIPPING SODA IN A COMBAT ZONE

Saturday night was a special night in our house. It was a night when the wife and I really made a production of our bedroom activities. That's not to say that Saturday night was the only night we made love, but Saturdays had a little extra *oomph*. Vicky emerged from the bathroom in a cloudy white teddy and posed in the doorway. Her long dark hair fell about her shoulders. The light from the bathroom illuminated her from behind, making her nightie all but disappear. I drank in the curves of her body with my eyes. On Saturdays, she always surprised me. She always topped herself.

"My, my," I said. The room was just about perfect. I lit the last candle and threw a handful of rose petals on the bed and then climbed into the silk sheets. "Get over here."

Vicky moved to me. She was slow and deliberate, such a tease. I rolled over, opened the nightstand and pulled out our mink glove. Vicky couldn't hold back her smile. She climbed into bed on all fours and started crawling towards me. We hadn't even touched yet, and I was ready to go. As she moved closer to me, her knee landed on the remote control. The TV came blaring on.

"Shit," she said.

"I'm sorry," I replied. "I didn't see the clicker when I put the sheets down."

"That totally killed my flow," she told me. Vicky sat down on the bed and leaned back on her elbows.

"I'll help you get it back," I told her and put the mink glove on. I slid my hand under her teddy and caressed her bare stomach, then ran the glove between her breasts. Usually the glove drove her wild, but I was getting nothing from her. I looked up for some sign of life. She wasn't paying any attention to me. Her gaze was locked straight ahead. "Time to turn the TV off," I said.

"Shhh," Vicky said and pointed to the TV.

I rolled over in a huff, annoyed that I had been shushed. It wasn't a regular shush either. I was shushed while making an advance. I was pissed. I looked at the television set. Martin Luther King, Jr. was on the screen. He was on the steps of the Lincoln Memorial giving a somewhat familiar but slightly altered speech. A colorful Peppie Cola bottle in Dr. King's hand stood out from the black and white footage. He raised the bottle in the air. The crowd broke into applause. "I have a dream."

"Isn't this sick?" Vicky asked without looking away from the eighty-inch plasma.

"I have a dream that one day Americans will be given an opportunity," an obviously dubbed Martin Luther King, Jr. spoke. The crowd hushed, solemn and serious. "An opportunity to tour the war-torn regions of the world and to drink Peppie Cola while doing so... I HAVE A DREAM!!!" Dr. King paused, nodded and then took a sip of his Peppie Cola. "I have a dream to see history firsthand and not watch it on TV. Now I may not get there with you, but thanks to Peppie Cola, fifteen lucky winners and their guest will. Play Peppie Cola's under-the-top game and win a once-in-a-lifetime trip to see war, as only some know it." Dr. King winked at the camera.

"We have to win that," Vicky turned to me. "Can you fix it so we can get on that trip?"

"I suppose," I said. "Wouldn't you rather go to the islands or Europe, maybe Dubai?"

"Absolutely not," she said. Vicky turned to me. She was as electric as a raw, exposed nerve. "Promise me you'll get us this trip. Promise me, promise me." She bounced on the bed.

"Alright," I said. "I promise."

"I want you to give it to me, really hard, right this second. Do it like you're mad at me." She pulled me on top of her. Say what you want about the idle rich, we're not idle in the sack.

I made a few phone calls the next day, traded in some favors. I would vote one way on this board and another way on that board. It was kind of sleazy, but these are the kinds of things we do, when we are in love. By the close of business, I had a name and a phone number: Tom Halprin of Akron, Ohio. I gave him a call, and we kicked around some numbers. I think we ended up with a mutually beneficial arrangement. He turned over his turn of the cap to me, and I gave him enough cash to buy a lake house for him and his family. Within the week, my wife and I were on our way to the combat zone with the rest of the Peppie Cola winners. We were flown over in a real army transport. Vicky and I were both excited. She started to jump in place once we stepped foot on the tarmac.

"You're so good to me," she said. Vicky put her arm in mine and leaned over to kiss my cheek.

"You deserve it," I told her. I was a little disappointed to find out that the inside of the transport had been remodeled with all the first-class amenities. That didn't seem to be in the spirit of this great adventure. When we went on safari, we slept in red dirt under the African sky. There was no luxury hotel built for us halfway up Everest. And the submersible wasn't retrofitted with lounge seats when we took it to the edge of the Marianas. Vicky kind of had this look on her face like "Are you serious?" I shrugged at her.

"Just roll with it, honey," I said. The plane's full compliment was relatively small. There looked to be no more than twenty of us. Vicky and I, just getting into our forties, seemed to be about the youngest winners. The couple sitting across from us seemed to be about ten years older than us, although they could've been our age. It was hard to tell. They didn't look like they took as good of care of themselves as Vicky and I did.

"Name's Eliot Wilson," I said and extended my hand across the aisle.

"Bob Mitchell." Bob grabbed my hand and gave me a more than firm shake. By the look of him he was a walking marshmallow, but judging by that handshake, I'd say he was made of steel. "This is my wife Nancy."

"Hi, Nancy," I said. "This is my wife Vicky."

"Aren't we just the luckiest?" Vicky asked. She leaned over my seat and extended her hand to Bob. "I mean, Eliot and I have been all over the world, but I don't think we've ever been a part of anything so unique."

"Well," Bob leaned towards us, "I've seen enough war in my day, but the little lady was the one to find our golden ticket, and the only way for me to be happy is to keep her happy."

"I hear you, Bob," I said. "I'd do just about anything for my little firecracker."

Our luck turned upon arrival. We landed at an American Army base somewhere off the desert shelf. Our accommodations were sparse and not very comfortable. We were assured that this was authentic to the combat experience. I slept terribly on a cot that smelled like a sock; it was wonderful. In the morning our tour gathered in the soldier's recreation hall for a get-to-know-your-group continental breakfast. A tiny but sturdily built man appeared at the head of the mess hall. He had dark hair and a pointy face. His green Peppie Cola corporate golf shirt popped in the otherwise blandly colored setting.

"Good afternoon, ladies and gents. My name is Steven, and I'll be your guide to the wonderful world of combat." He flashed us a bright smile and gave a big rainbow-arched wave.

"Before I get started, there are a few questions I have to ask, just a formality." Steven held his hands together, took a breath and then continued. "Is anyone here currently a member of or had any affiliation with any militant groups with anti-American agendas?" The crowd sat silently for a moment. "Great, any Jews?" My wife turned to me and slowly mouthed, "*What the fuck?*" I was at a loss. "Relax, I'm kidding," Steven continued. "Kind of, but seriously, if you're Jewish, you'll want to watch yourself on some of our stops. Any questions?"

"Are you a hundred percent sure we are going to be safe on this trip?" Vicky asked.

"Almost a hundred percent sure." Steven clapped his hands together, then moved to the next point. "Okay, let's take a look at our transportation." Steven moved aside as the curtain behind him opened. The lights went down and the picture came up. "This is your Carnage Caravan," he announced.

"The Carnage Caravan represents the pinnacle of recreational automotive excellence." The black screen turned to a desert landscape, barren and rocky. The camera zoomed along a black two-lane highway. The rumble of an engine became audible and then the reveal: the Carnage Caravan was a hulk of a double-decker bus, jet black, with muscular curves running down its side. "Every seat is handcrafted and designed to give you maximum comfort," Steven continued to narrate.

"Each passenger will have their own television with satellite hook-up," he added. "You will have exclusive access to some of the behind-the-scenes, real-time war negotiations. There's more to this conflict than what happens on the battlefield. We put you in the middle of the action in every conceivable way." The Peppie logo appeared on the screen and Steven retook center stage.

"Alright, people, this is what we've been waiting for. Let's get our little tushies on that bus and check out the combat zone everyone's talking about." Steven walked down the aisle between our tables towards the exit. "Everybody up." He turned and waved us on. "Follow me, folks. It all starts now."

"Jesus, that's a big sucker," Bob said as he stepped out of the mess hall. The Carnage Caravan was rumbling angrily as it sat idle outside the mess hall. It was a true behemoth, utterly impractical and completely awesome. A six-foot Peppie Cola bottle with arms and legs appeared from the entrance of the Carnage Caravan.

"What in God's name is that?" Bob asked.

"This is Percy, the Peppie Cola bottle," Steven interjected. "He'll be our mascot as we travel through the hell on Earth that is combat."

"That's the damnedest thing I've ever seen," Bob replied.

Percy made his way through the group shaking hands and giving out hugs.

"Just ease your way to the back of the Carnage Caravan, and you'll find the stairs to the obse. ation deck," Steven informed the tour group.

"This thing is amazing," I told my wife. We entered the belly of the great tour bus, which was set up much like a lounge. The décor wasn't all that different from one of those swank clubs in the Meatpacking District. Bob and Nancy followed us to the back where we took a spiral staircase to the top of the recreational tank. The bus' second floor was encased bulletproof glass. It allowed us a three-hundred-and-sixty-degree vantage of the area. Add that to our height, which I bet was about fourteen feet off the ground, and it seemed like we could see for miles.

"Let's all take our seats!" Steven stood at the front of the observation deck; he was careful to have a moment of eye contact with each one of us as he spoke. "I'd like to take this time to go over some of the rules. If you look under your seat, you will find a list of Do's and Don't's while traveling through a hostile zone. Please refrain from making any obscene or otherwise lewd gestures to any of the non-combatants. Remember: we are guests in their horror.

"In the unlikely event of a ground war, rip the cloth off your headrest and fasten it to your arm so the words 'U.N. Official' are prominently displayed. For added safety, your seat will become a bulletproof vest. We would also ask you not to feed any hostiles." A disapproving sigh emanated from the tourists. "Don't worry, you'll all have the chance to work in an actual Red Cross food line at a pre-designated safe zone. And finally the most import rule of all: have fun!"

By the time Percy, the Peppie Bottle, finished handing out peanuts, the Carnage Caravan was already at the border. We were only miles from the hot zone. I flipped through the TV channels and found two men negotiating in a small room. Each man had a different miniature flag pitched in front of them. Despite being locked in the throes of war, the two seemed to be engaged in a rather cordial discussion.

"Listen, guy," the man in dark gray said to the man in the light gray suit, "you've got to promise me that you're not going to hit any of our petrochemical plants."

"You have to be kidding, buddy," the man in light gray replied. "Those are great targets for us. We cripple your infrastructure and minimize casualties. It's win/win."

"Guy, come on. Do you know how much those things cost us? Plus, they are a bitch to rebuild. Here is the address of a condo highrise that is ninety-nine percent complete. Blow the shit out of it. Minimal collateral damage, and there will be great TV coverage of it. I'll have my people put, like, four cameras on it."

"And what do I get out of it?"

"We'll keep maintaining that our guidance chips don't work on our rockets, which you know is bullshit. Plus, we'll purposely stay away from heavily populated areas."

"Speaking of which, everyone is pissed you hit that graveyard with a rocket."

"I know, guy. Sorry about that." The man in the dark gray suit took out a cigarette and lit it. "Were there any survivors?"

"I walked into that one," the man in light gray chuckled. "Your petrochemical plants are safe."

Once the talks went to commercial, I started flipping around again. Vicky, as she always does on vacation, read through the local travel books. I stumbled onto a channel that split the monitor into several screens. It appeared to be the security feed from the cameras mounted on the exterior of the bus.

"Hey, Steven." I raised my hand.

"Yes, Mr. Wilson." Steven touched my shoulder, gave me a big smile, and then wrinkled his brow. "What can I do for you?"

"I'm just looking at the monitor here, and it looks like the road ahead is blocked by some people." Steven leaned down on one knee and looked at my TV. "They look pretty worse for wear. Can we offer a hand?"

"I think that would be a violation of our treaty," Steven said. "You see, we are here strictly as observers. We are representatives of the Peppie Cola Corporation and cannot jeopardize their corporate neutrality."

"Steven," I said, "these people, they're devastated."

"If someone blew up the place where you kept your family, you'd be pretty devastated, too. But don't worry about it. You're safe and sound in the Carnage Caravan. Securetech spared no expense when they built this baby. The exterior has an electrified hull that sends a series of electric currents into anyone who comes into contact with it. That way we can avoid being mobbed by hordes of refugees who have gone mad with fear."

"You're going to electrocute refugees?" Vicky asked.

"That's a keeper," the old woman sitting in front of us said. She had leaned over her husband and snapped a picture of some children digging through the wreckage of a bombed house.

"Can we stop the bus and get out?" the elderly husband asked. I remembered meeting him on the plane ride over. He told me he and his wife were retired and lived in Texas.

"Of course, we can, but don't stray too far," Steven said. "Anyone interested in a little field trip can follow me. We're going to meet a family that has been devastated by a recent bombing."

"Are you sure it's safe?" Vicky asked again.

"Aren't you a little worry wart? Adorable." Steven pinched her cheek. "Eyes front, people." Steven spoke into a microphone connected to a portable amplifier attached to his belt. "What you're seeing here is a family picking through the ruins of what was once their home. In all likelihood, these people are now living like animals. They are probably surviving on refuse, vermin and plant matter. Most likely they are forced to go to the bathroom in the streets or holes dug in the ground."

"I speak English," the father of the family said. "I know what you are saying about us."

"Well, we lucked out people," Steven announced. "It looks like this one speaks English."

"I went to university in London."

"Sir," Steven said, putting his hand on the man's shoulder. "Are you now forced to eat garbage and pee in the streets?"

The gentleman did not reply. He stared with his mouth open.

"This gives me a great idea," Steven said. "Percy, get over here and get next to the family."

"What's wrong with you people?" the father asked. "This was our home, my family has nothing left. Have some respect. For God's sake, we are people."

The young boy broke from his father's side, picked up a rock, and threw it at the bus. His frustrated gesture did little to curb the curiosity of our group. We started to steer clear of the family, but a couple people couldn't help themselves and continued snapping pictures. After all, this is what Peppie Cola brought us to see. I took Vicky by the hand and led her towards a bomb crater. We walked to the bottom of it, the center of the impact. The devastation was total, eerie and magnificent.

"Wait up, guys," Bob called after us. He and Nancy negotiated the uneven rubble.

"Do you hear that?" Nancy said. She and Bob stopped at the ridge of the crater and looked around.

"What is that?" Vicky asked. It seemed to be the sound of firecrackers in the distance.

"Now I hear a whistling," Nancy said.

"Yup, I hear that," Bob answered. He looked around as the whistle rose in pitch. I started to walk up the crater towards them. Bob locked in on the sound and looked straight up above him. The whistle stopped, there was an explosion, and then he and Nancy disappeared in a cloud of smoke and rubble. I was knocked off my feet and everything went black.

When I came to, I heard screaming but couldn't see anything. I tried to open my eyes. They stung. The smell of burnt flesh was strong in my nose. I carefully put my fingers to my eyes. They were gone. My eye sockets were just meaty patches of dead flesh, not even registering my touch.

"I'm blind," I screamed.

Vicky grabbed my arm and pulled me towards the Carnage Caravan. "You're going to be fine," Vicky reassured me. "You're not blind. You have penis all over your face."

I felt a release of suction as my sight returned. My wife held Bob's penis by the tip, between her thumb and forefinger. The scrotum, which had been butterflied open, must have smacked me in the head and covered the top of my face like a perverted mask. We stumbled to the caravan amid heavy explosions. My shoulder felt raw with ache, and I was bleeding quite a bit.

"I think I've been hit," I said.

"Bob," Nancy screamed. "Bob, I can't find my arms." Nancy stumbled towards us, a badly burned torso with a head and legs. "Can you help me? I've lost my arms."

"Hold on, Nancy. We'll help," I said.

Vicky started to turn me, but we were too late. Another mortar hit ripped Nancy to bits. She was gone.

"What do we do, Steven?" my wife yelled.

"Okay, people. Listen up. The noise you are hearing is gunfire interspersed with mortar hits. The good news is this is not a military action." He talked as he waved us into the Caravan. "The bad news is it is probably a gang of lawless, well-armed thugs robbing and raping their way across the city. So please everyone mind your step."

"Steven's going to get us killed," Vicky said as she helped me into a seat on the lower level of the bus.

"I'm getting a little light-headed, honey," I said. "I think I'm bleeding pretty bad."

"We've got to get moving," she told me. "We're not going to end up like Bob and Nancy."

"Goddamn!" Steven exclaimed. Mortars exploded next to the bus, causing the hulking caravan to rock. "I didn't think we were going to see live action. Who wants a Peppie Cola?"

Steven bit into the side of an unopened can. He looked like a vampire feasting on a neck. Soda fizzed and sprayed from the punctures. Once he drained the liquid, he crushed the can, dropped it to the ground. Steven wiped his mouth, then turned and followed the last contest winner inside the bus.

The Carnage Caravan was smacked by a direct hit. The nice older couple from Texas tumbled down the staircase in a ball of fire. Their screams rang dull in my ears, and my nose filled with the smell of their burning bodies. Vicky grabbed a fire extinguisher and started to put them out. It was useless. By the time she got the fire out, the old couple looked to be nothing more than a crispy pile of clothes melted over cooked beef.

"Goddamn it, get this bus moving," Vicky called out.

The engine roared on and we rolled out of the area. We were lucky that this stop was only a few short miles from the Red Cross Safe Zone. I started to sweat. The pain from the shrapnel hit was nearly unbearable.

"Alright, folks. We're here!" Steven stated over the loud speaker. "I just want to say to all the survivors, nice work. You stayed alert and that kept you alive. Now, I'm going to give you a quick tour through the camp, and then you will be given an hour to explore on your own and seek medical attention. Don't forget your name tags."

We gathered outside the bus for Steven to make a head count. Tents stretched out for miles. Thousands of disheveled people stood in food lines in the middle of the camp. Others crowded around small fires and listened to handheld radios. The smell of shit and death filled the air.

"This is horrible," Vicky said. "I can't believe this is really happening."

"Take it easy, honey. They'll be alright."

"Don't fret, Mrs. Wilson," Steven said. "These people are used to it."

"You're an unbelievably dense asshole," Vicky told Steven.

Steven shrugged and turned to the survivors. "We are short a few travelers. Does anyone know who's missing?"

"This is all that's left of Bob." I pulled his member out of my pocket and showed it to Steven.

"Right." Steven crossed a name off his clipboard. "We're still one person short. Not counting the two burnt corpses and Nancy. Who's missing a partner?"

"Dear God," Vicky said. She went white with disbelief.

I took my wife in my good arm and looked over her head.

"What kind of person is capable of such heinous acts?" I asked my wife.

"Amazing," Steven said, wide-eyed.

The thugs' convoy barreled into the Red Cross Safe Zone. The lead truck had Percy, the Peppie Cola bottle, strapped to its hood. I knew he was still alive because his arms and legs were flailing about. The convoy pulled up to a tree that stood at the edge of the Red Cross base. The thugs emptied out of their trucks and grabbed Percy off the hood, then dragged him by his bottle top. One soldier threw rope over a branch while another fashioned the end to Percy's neck. It took five thugs to get him in the air.

Since the rope was tied around the neck of the Peppie Cola bottle costume, he was in no danger of strangulation. A savage beating in the form of a human-piñata game began. The thugs grew bored.

One of the men took aim at Percy and fired. The bullet hole dotted the small *i* of the Peppie brand name. Percy's kicking legs stopped and hung limp. In a last heartless act, they cut him down and urinated on his corpse.

"He never broke character," Steven said softly.

The thugs chuckled and congratulated one another. One lit a cigarette and looked in our direction. He tapped the shoulder of a bigger fellow and pointed towards us. "Check them out, boss."

The big fellow nodded and waved the rest of the thugs along with him. They moved towards us, guns trained on our group.

"I can't feel my arm," I told my wife.

"It's cold," she said, holding my hand.

"You're beautiful," I told her.

She looked at me, and I could see it in her face. She knew how much I meant it. She told me she loved me. She said she loved me and that's all that would ever matter.

C O D A

There is a silent unmoving pile of bodies that fills the living room. They lay where they have fallen, still wearing the clothes they had on last night. I am sure they have had a good night out and I am glad for them. I don't feel much like sleeping, and wouldn't even if there were room. I walk out onto the beach. The sun is on the rise but still only hovering above the water; already it is heating up the day. Salt air smells nice, and cool sand feels good when I squish it between my toes. That's about all I can claim to know about what goes on. But sometimes I imagine other places. Sometimes I wonder what it's like out in the desert. I think about the heat and the moments that make up your life. I wonder how many times you think about death each day, how many people you've killed. But I can only think that for a short time before I have to push those thoughts out of my mind.

ACKNOWLEDGEMENTS

Big thanks to the publishing force that is Jackie Corley. Without her, this collection would not be. Thanks to the editors who have nudged me along by publishing my work. I am grateful for the help given to me by my father, The Drake, The Terrell family, and everyone else who took time to look over these stories. Special thanks go to James Rahn and the Rittenhouse Writers' Group for their invaluable insights, observations and criticism. —*TW*

ABOUT THE AUTHOR

Timmy Waldron is native to the humid subtropical climate of New Jersey. He is a fiction editor for *Word Riot* and has been published in many online and print journals. You can find him on Facebook, or email him at timmywaldron@gmail.com.